He climbed
They picked the
the stream. Jak
pillowed his hea

trumpet-shaped Jessamine above them. Claire settled in beside him, and gazed into the gently flowing water. Tiny lavender wildflowers no bigger than raindrops were sprinkled along the water's edge. Claire picked a miniature bouquet as Jake continued to lay still and quiet, looking up at the golden tangle of blooms.

"I bet we're the only people who've ever seen this. Paw doesn't come this far out when he goes hunting," Claire said.

She rearranged the delicate wildflowers held between her thumb and forefinger and tossed them into the water. They dispersed and drifted away as she let the water ripple between her fingers. She leaned back and looked into the flowers draped above them. "It seems like a waste, doesn't it? For all this to be hidden away and only us getting to see it. If you hadn't found it, it would've bloomed and died and no one would've ever known it was here."

Jake looked steadily at her and said, "If eyes were made for seeing, then beauty is its own excuse for being."

She turned onto her elbow and faced him with a puzzled expression. "What?"

"Ralph Waldo Emerson," he replied, rolling onto his side and looking back at her.

"Ohhh," she said, softly. "I thought maybe that was something you'd just made up."

He looked into her wide green eyes. "I wish."

Come Round Right

by

Sarah C. Goodman

To April —

Sarah Goodman

Come Round Right

Cover Art by *Kim Mendoza*

The Wild Rose Press
PO Box 708
Adams Basin, NY 14410-0706
Visit us at www.thewildrosepress.com

Publishing History
First White Rose Edition, 2007
Print ISBN 1-60154-120-1

Published in the United States of America

Dedication

To Johnny and Thelma
for believing

To Jeff…
"Love Never Fails"

Chapter One

"That's quite a scar, Mrs. Nugent." Claire Burke hoped her tone expressed the awe her patient was hoping for instead of the amusement she was actually feeling. She was staring at the pasty, pale midsection of an eighty-year-old woman who was brazenly baring her belly and saying, "Ain't that something?"

Mrs. Nugent continued her story with gusto. "I was sitting on the couch, watching *Wheel of Fortune*, when, lo and behold, my appendix ruptured. If I hadn't got to the hospital so quick I might've passed on. My pastor was over for a visit when it happened and he drove me. The good Lord was watching out for me and this scar is my souvenir to prove it."

Claire nodded in agreement and commented again that it was quite an impressive scar. "Um, the doctor did a nice job sewing you up."

Her nursing teachers had instructed their students to show empathy with patients, but Claire wasn't really sure how to respond to this show-and-tell story. Mrs. Lola Faye Nugent continued holding her gown aloft and nodding solemnly while Claire finished making notes on a chart. It was even harder not to laugh considering her elderly patient was in the hospital this particular day for treatment of a broken hip. Mrs. Nugent didn't have a legitimate reason to have her gown wadded up around her neck. Claire tried to suppress a grin. *I'm getting this little peep-show just because she loves telling the story of the scar.* Claire had developed a soft spot for the slightly eccentric, older lady. With her ball of white hair and half-glasses, she reminded Claire of her grandmother. *Except Gran would die before she showed off her belly to anyone other than Paw.*

Claire blew on her stethoscope to warm it before she checked Mrs. Nugent's heart rate. Her mind drifted to the little house in the country with a porch running all the way

1

across the front and rocking chairs waiting for company to come. It was so different from her own home in its perfectly groomed subdivision. She was looking forward to seeing Gran and Paw again. It had been too long.

While Claire finished checking her vitals, Mrs. Nugent continued to chatter away. "I'll be glad to get home tomorrow. I've been out of church for two weeks now. Do you go to church, Honey?"

"Yes, Ma'am," Claire replied. "I go to First Community Church downtown."

"How do you keep from getting lost in that big ol' thing? I used to go to a church in Pickens, but when they started singing all one part and putting the words up on a projector screen, I decided to move on. If you don't have a hymnal to hold, you don't have anything to do with your hands except hold 'em up in the air and that just ain't for me. Do you like hymns?"

Not waiting for an answer, the broken-hipped, but not broken-tongued, octogenarian continued. "For the last few years, I've been going to a little, bitty, country church. It's been like a family to me, especially since my Bud died."

"I'm glad you found a church home that suits you," Claire said as she finished making notes on her patient's chart. "You take care, Mrs. Nugent. I won't be seeing you after today. This is my last day of clinicals and after finals next week, I'll be done with my training."

After four years of nursing school, Claire was aching to get school work and rotations behind her and find her first real job. A real job, far away from Little Rock, preferably in the biggest city she could find.

"Congratulations, Honey. What will you do now? Work here, I reckon?"

"No, I think I'm going to see some more of the world, get a taste of big-city life. I'll start applying for jobs in places that look interesting and see what turns up."

Mrs. Nugent considered this as she looked out at the lines of traffic zigzagging along below the window. "Good luck, Sugar. Little Rock is plenty big enough for me. I've never even liked coming up *here*, especially during rush hour. You can't get across that River Bridge without someone trying to run you over!"

"Well, maybe I'll end up somewhere with taxis and I'll

let a cabbie do the dodging and weaving for me," Claire remarked.

"To each her own, I guess. I'll sure miss seeing you. Don't tell the other nurses, but you were my favorite."

"Well, don't tell the other patients, but you were my favorite, too," Claire replied with a grin as she backed away from the bed.

She was almost to the door before she turned and didn't see the tall, slender man coming in until she'd bumped right into him. Her up-turned nose was squashed flat against his chest for a split second before she bounced backward in alarm, her clipboard clattering to the floor.

"Let me get that," as he stooped to retrieve it for her.

When he straightened up, Claire noticed he was around six feet tall, with a lanky build. Claire looked up to thank him, then apologized in rapid fire succession. "Thank you...I'm sorry...thank you...I'm sorry." Then she threw in a few more for good measure. "I'm sorry. Really. Very sorry." It wasn't exactly sparkling conversation but it was the best she could do in that mortifying moment. She looked down, trying to will the flush of embarrassment off her cheeks. *Why isn't there ever a hole in the floor when you need one?*

"Really, it's no problem," he replied, with a distinct drawl. The voice was so soothing, so welcoming and warm Claire couldn't resist looking at him.

Hazel eyes, with honey colored flecks in them. These particular eyes were kind, with a barely contained spark of mischief. Claire guessed he was in his late twenties, although the wide smile and sandy-brown hair gave him a boyish quality, as did his rolled up shirt sleeves. She noticed he was perfectly at ease, something rare in a hospital room.

Claire was suddenly very aware of hair which was escaping her ponytail in fuzzy wisps and that her makeup had probably worn off by now.

She finally managed to produce a semi-intelligent sentence. "I should watch where I'm going. I do apologize."

"I noticed," he said with a grin. The blush that had just started to die down blazed up in an instant, shading her pale skin crimson all the way to her hairline. She pushed the door open and hurried through it. As it swung shut, she heard Mrs. Nugent say, "Brother Jake, I'm so glad to see you."

Claire hurried down the hall, thinking about those hazel eyes. She was still trying to wrestle her hair back into place as she stepped into the solitary safety of the elevator.

****

By the time she slid into the driver's seat of her burgundy Camry and pulled out of the parking lot, Claire felt a little more composed. This wasn't the first ditzy thing she'd done at the hospital, she reminded herself with a rueful half-smile. On the first day of clinicals, she had tried to stop off at a water fountain for a quick drink without her instructor noticing she was gone from the group. The fountain had an overly sensitive handle and her chance of subtlety was lost when she showered the entire right side of her head. Since then, she'd steered clear of the third-floor fountain she'd dubbed Old Faceful.

Turning her attention to the midday traffic, Claire maneuvered skillfully along Interstate 30 and found her exit. She didn't mind the traffic as much as Mrs. Nugent did, but she was glad to see the four lanes narrow to two as she left Little Rock behind. Her grandparents' farm was waiting, and so was Gran's good cooking.

Claire wound down the highway toward the little community of Dogwood. The houses grew sparse and scattered as the fields and pastures began to outnumber them. It was haymaking time again in Arkansas for those farmers who were lucky enough to have a second cutting. Cows dotted the landscape on both sides of the highway and Claire couldn't help admiring the frolicking calves. She wondered if Paw had any new calves. He'd always let her name them and she had delighted in trailing after him in the pale light of daybreak to check on the herd. The summers she spent with her grandparents held some of her fondest memories, preserved in her mind in the yellow glow of sunshine and hayfields.

A little frown creased Claire's high forehead as she drove. Her grandparents were supposed to be retired, but they still kept about twenty-five cows and one cantankerous, old bull named Charles. She worried they did too much, worked too hard for people who were in the "evening of life," as Gran described it.

Still, Claire was relieved Paw had at least slowed down and given up running two hundred head of beef cattle. She could remember seeing their sleek, shining backs lined up at the feeders as they contentedly munched their grain. Claire's frown shifted into a look of exasperated affection as she recalled asking Gran if the cows knew they were going to be made into steaks and hamburgers.

"Oh no, Angel," Gran had replied to her young granddaughter, "but they like it better that way. You can't enjoy your feed if you know you'll be on the wrong side of the trough sooner or later."

It's a miracle I'm not a vegetarian now. Or maybe it's Gran's pot roast. Claire turned on Highway 291 South and started the last leg of her trip. The one stoplight town of Pickens was about twenty miles behind her when she finally saw her grandparents' place, perched on the side of a highway that had been nothing but a gravel road when they'd moved there fifty years before.

Claire pulled into the yard and parked her car under a sweet gum tree with a sigh of relief. The Burke farm looked wonderfully unchanged since her last visit four years ago.

Gran appeared at the front door, wiping her hands on an apron and calling, "Claire, you better move that car or the mockingbirds will decorate it for you!" Claire ignored the advice and rushed forward to hug her grandmother. Gran was still fussing about "those blame mockingbirds," as she led Claire onto the porch and pointed to a weathered porch swing. "You sit there, Sugar." Gran looked once more at her Camry in the yard, "If you ain't gonna move your car, you can't say I didn't warn you when you find a mess on your hood in the morning."

"Gran, I haven't seen you since I started nursing school. I'd rather talk to you than worry about the car. Why don't you sit down and catch me up on what you and Paw have been doing?" Claire had been taking summer classes since she started college and had neglected her usual trips to Dogwood. Her goal was to get out of college as fast as possible and get on with real life. When Claire had said as much to Gran before she started school, Gran had peered over her half-glasses and remarked, "Honey, you don't have to rush all the time. Sometimes, you get in such a hurry, you're not even sure where you're runnin' or why. You're just runnin' for its own sake."

No one would ever accuse Gran of mincing words. Gran

eased down next to Claire. Her grandmother preferred they not move at all while they sat. Claire always said it should be called a "porch-hang" at the home of Millie and Franklin Burke.

As Gran settled back, careful not to move the swing, she patted Claire's hand. "You want to know what me and Paw have been up to? We're just fiddling with these cows and living life, I guess. Your Paw's got a garden, but the bugs have about eaten it up. I did get enough new potatoes dug for supper. You like them boiled with a little butter, don't you?"

"You know I do, Gran. But I'm going to have to nag you about all this cooking with butter, lard and shortening since I'm almost a fully, certified, health-care professional now," Claire teased.

"Shoot, Claire. You better not say anything to your Paw about leaving the good stuff out of the food. He'll just say, 'Well, I'm gonna die of something someday. I might as well enjoy life while I'm alive.'"

"You better not be running your mouth about me to my baby girl, Millie." Paw came around the corner, wearing gum boots, a dilapidated, straw hat, and his ever present Big Smith overalls. He was carrying several crooked-neck squash and a few zucchini as well.

Claire looked at his sweat-soaked face. "Paw, didn't the doctor tell you to take it easy?" Paw had taken a tumble off the farmhouse roof while replacing the shingles a few months ago, but he insisted he was none the worse for wear.

Paw snorted. "Me and him have different ideas of easy. Feel these hands." He stepped up onto the porch and held out a leathered paw for Claire to examine. "About as soft as a baby's rear." His palm was still a solid callous, no matter what he said to the contrary. Claire looked at him skeptically. Paw leaned forward and said in a loud whisper, "I'll be as soft as your Gran before much longer if I don't watch out." Paw hurried into the house before Gran had time to respond, with Claire following hard on his heels.

"Franklin, I better not hear any more of that mouth of yours or you'll be eating cold cereal for supper tonight," Gran said as she followed them.

After supper, Claire sat on the porch swing, listening to the whippoorwills and crickets combine their music into a summer night symphony. Twilight drifted down slowly, coming to rest on the fog-blanketed pastures. The land was bedded down for the night. She breathed in the scent of honeysuckle and exhaled. Her neck and shoulders began to relax as knots of tension she hadn't even known were there ebbed away. Claire sat on the swing, wonderfully still both inside and out, until the hum of mosquitoes sent her inside to the comfort of a goose-down pillow and a patchwork quilt.

****

Claire fumbled for her alarm, trying to shut out the screeching sound that had jarred her awake. It took a minute for her to clear her head and realize the harsh, raucous racket was outside. In her grogginess, she couldn't quite identify the makers of the noise, and before she got a handle on what she was hearing the sound changed again. Now a trilling song filtered in through the windows.

Mockingbirds, annoyed she tried to block out the din by placing a pillow over her head. Almost smothering herself wasn't accomplishing anything, so she got up with a yawn and made her way to the kitchen.

Gran was puttering around, making bacon, eggs, and real biscuits. Claire always called them real biscuits, because they involved flour and other ingredients being mixed together. They weren't the kind that came in a can and only required being whacked on the counter, opened and cooked.

"I was fixin' to come wake you up," Gran commented. She was wearing a house dress and slippers that had to have at least twenty years of shuffling about the little house to their credit. "Church starts at eleven. You did bring Sunday clothes, didn't you?"

Still somewhat groggy and more than a little miffed at the mockingbirds, Claire nodded and began to slather strawberry jelly on a biscuit. "Where's Paw?"

"In the tub." A sloshing sound came from the back of the house. When Paw emerged from the bathroom smelling strongly of Old Spice, Claire gathered her toiletries and took her turn in the small bathroom.

She decided the well water must have some kind of voodoo power over her hair. After sweating under the blow dryer for thirty minutes trying to get her thick, wavy locks completely dried and straightened, Claire finally gave up.

Maybe it was the evil humidity. Whatever the cause, it was going to be another ponytail day. The curly halo of auburn that escaped and shone around her head made her look like a cross between an angel and an elf.

"I look about sixteen years old," she grumbled. Reaching for her makeup, she highlighted her green eyes with brown liner and mascara. *Green eyes don't get enough press.* There were songs galore about blue eyes and the enchanting girls who owned them. There are even a few brown-eyed-girl songs. Green, though, was overlooked. *I've always liked my eyes.* The hair was another story. With a sigh, she headed for the car where her grandparents waited.

Gran and Paw had owned three white Buicks in a row and this particular one for at least fifteen years. Claire remembered riding in it when she was a little girl. It still smelled faintly of Avon dusting powder and peppermints, the kind Paw always kept with him to hand out to children who were brave enough to face his imposing form and hold out their sticky hands.

Claire slid into the backseat and watched as the fields began to slip past outside her window.

"Looks like the Culpeppers have a new bull. Charolais, isn't it?" Gran was an expert on cattle breeds. She often accompanied Paw to the stockyard when he was going to buy more cows. He didn't need her advice, as he'd made clear plenty of times, but she felt obliged to offer it nonetheless.

"Cross-breed, I reckon," Paw remarked.

"Oh, it is not, Franklin. Look at the size of them ears!" They scuffled about the distinguishing marks of Charolais cattle for a while until the conversation went on about this person's garden and that one's hay.

As they talked, Claire looked at her grandfather in the rearview mirror. She was struck by how much her father resembled him. The same, heavy brows over piercing, blue eyes, wide shoulders, and broad hands with flat fingernails but her dad's hands had never been as calloused as Paw's.

While Franklin Monroe Burke Jr., F. Monroe Burke to his associates and clients, shared his father's tireless work ethic, he didn't share his love of the land or the country life. He called it "*manual* labor." It wasn't the words but the tone that gave away his feelings. Claire remembered him saying he'd taken the first chance he had to follow the red dirt road out of Dogwood. Corporate law was something Millie and Frank, Sr. knew nothing about, but they were still very proud of their son for being a success in his field. They only wished he'd call and come to visit them more often. Even after Claire's mother died, he had come back to Dogwood only to drop Claire off and pick her up again.

"Come on, kiddo," he'd say. "Let's get out of the sticks and back to civilization."

She stared absently as they drove along the pothole-sprinkled highway. She decided she'd ask her advisor to dig up a few potential job leads when she went to take her finals next week.

"I need to make a motion to buy a new flag for the flagpole at the next business meeting. That one's looking ragged." Paw's voice broke into Claire's daydreaming. She was surprised to see they'd arrived at Dogwood Community Church.

Claire stepped out of the car and onto the white gravel parking lot. She had forgotten this little house of God was not much larger than a decent sized family home. There were no stained glass windows or other adornments. The only things to distinguish it from a residential home were the white steeple perched on its roof and the long fellowship hall attached to the rear of the building by a covered walkway.

All around the church, people were piling out of cars and pickups coated in the dirt of Grant County's unpaved roads. Young families with babies and elderly members alike stopped to greet each other on the narrow porch. It seemed like some silent church bells had sounded that only the Dogwood members could hear, signaling them to gather for worship. The parking lot, which had been empty when the Burkes arrived, filled up almost instantly as people filtered into the church.

Claire followed her grandparents, who stopped to talk with just about everyone on their way into the building. Once inside, they made their way to the same pew they'd occupied for decades, third row from the back, left side. They slid to the end of the pew and Claire did the same. She noticed most of the oak pews had dark patches on their backs, as if they were stained with something. Leaning over to check the spot behind her grandmother, she realized the discolorations were worn places. The same backs had leaned against the same pews for so long, the wood had been stained. She could even make out tiny bits of fabric from who knows how many years of Sunday finery embedded in the grain of the wood.

Looking around the church at groups of people talking about this one's new grandbaby and that one's gall bladder surgery, Claire was suddenly struck by how much the scene resembled a big family reunion.

The song director, a man with a lot of chin and not a lot of hair, stepped up onto the platform where the pulpit stood. His presence quieted the building immediately.

"Good morning, folks. Glad to see such a good number here today." Claire took a quick mental count. She guessed there were about sixty people in the building. "Everyone take your red hymnals and we'll sing number 325."

As the strains of "At the Cross" drifted from the upright piano, Claire listened to voices rising around the church. Some were melodic and wonderful to hear; others were beautiful only to God.

Since Claire thought her version of making a joyful noise unto the Lord consisted of too much noise and not much joy, she didn't join in the singing. Instead, she practiced one of her favorite hobbies—people watching.

Directly in front of her was a young couple with two small girls and a world of baby paraphernalia piled between them. It appeared taking two children to church required the mobilization skills of an army general. Standing amid the baby dolls, blankies, and burp rags, while peering over the pew back, was a tiny girl with startlingly blue eyes who Claire guessed to be about a year old. Her precious few wisps of corn silk hair were captured tenuously in a white bow that refused to stay put. Her sister, who was contentedly slurping apple juice from a sticky looking sippy-cup and munching on animal crackers, was around three-years-old. Their mother had to continually remind her eldest daughter in whispered tones to keep her feet off the pew.

You always hear about the patience of Job, but it is the patience of a mother that's truly miraculous, Claire smiled as the mother searched for her youngest child's pacifier on the floor for the fifth time. Seeing it was under her pew, Claire retrieved it and tapped the woman on the shoulder. As she took the pacifier back with a grateful smile, Claire was surprised to see she was about her own age. *She already has two children. I bet she has some stories to tell.* The young woman mouthed her thanks; stuck the pacifier, which was now of questionable cleanliness, back in the baby's mouth and turned around to share a hymnal with her husband.

Claire's eyes wandered around the sanctuary. The congregation had a large percentage of older members along with a sprinkling of young families and a few teenagers holding down the back pew. Besides the couple in front of her, she didn't see any other folks her own age except one young woman who just didn't strike her right.

She occupied a middle pew along the middle aisle. In Claire's opinion, this girl was just *too...* Her makeup was too...perfect, her gleaming brunette hair was too...coifed, her smile and manner too...polished and practiced. She was wearing an obviously expensive suit, large audacious earrings, and ankle-breaking high heels. Claire noticed she kept a smile on her face the entire time she sang. *Now how in the world do you sing and smile at the same time?* The perfect girl, whom she'd dubbed Miss Dogwood America, kept looking at someone on the far, left side of the church. Claire couldn't see who she was looking at, but she certainly turned the wattage of her blindingly white smile up a few notches whenever she glanced in that direction.

The song director asked, "Are there any prayer requests today?"

A voice from the back said, "Brother Wells, I'd like to thank everyone for praying for me when I was in the hospital and for bringing over all the food when I came home. I didn't have to cook for a week. I've got some of the dishes in the car so y'all can get them after church. Could you all please pray for my neighbor's daughter's husband's niece. She's having surgery tomorrow. I don't know her name, or where her surgery is, or what's wrong with her, but the Lord will."

The song director looked a touch bemused, but not at all surprised, by this vague request. "Please remember to mention this one in your prayers. Thank you, Mrs. Lola Faye."

Claire craned her neck to see her former patient standing with the aid of a walker, but otherwise looking as fit and fine as an eighty-year-old woman can look.

"Gran," she whispered, "that lady was one of my patients."

"Well, you've met one of a kind," Gran replied. "Lola Faye Nugent is a feisty lady. She doesn't have the foggiest notion she's old. Even goes to the nursing home on Mondays to help the elderly." Gran's story was cut short by a reproving glance from Paw, who didn't like the slightest noise during services.

"If there are no further announcements or prayer requests, then we'll turn the services over to Brother Jake," said Mr. Wells.

Claire was still thinking what a small world it was when she realized small wasn't the right word. Tiny was more like it. Situating his papers and preparing to deliver the morning sermon was the man from the hospital, Mr. Honey-Eyes himself, Brother Jake Weston.

Chapter Two

Jake Weston settled in behind the pulpit with a friendly grin. "Morning, Everyone. Welcome to Dogwood Community Church." His gaze swept across the congregation. When he spotted Claire, he looked genuinely pleased. "We're happy to see visitors here today. Home folks, please make our visitors feel welcome after services. Don't let them get away without at least a handshake."

Upon being the direct recipient of the preacher's smile, Claire felt her ears warming so she knew she must be blushing again. Chiding herself for reacting like a thirteen-year-old at a junior high dance, Claire gave what she hoped was a polite, closed-lip smile in return.

From the corner of her eye, Claire noticed Miss Dogwood America seemed to have developed some sort of seizure in her neck. Seated directly in front of Brother Weston, she was continually tossing her long, shiny hair over her shoulders and back again. Brother Weston seemed completely oblivious to this odd malady, and furthermore didn't seem to notice her smile intensity had moved up to "stun."

During the sermon, it was easy for Claire to pay attention. Brother Weston was an engaging speaker and his sermon seemed tailored just for her.

"Today, I'm going to talk about finding the will of God for your life. We have this idea that life is something like Robert Frost's poem, 'The Road Not Taken'. There are two roads diverging in a yellow wood, and we're supposed to pick the *one* that is 'God's plan'. This job is God's will, not that one; God wants me to go to this college, not that one. One path is God's will, one is not. That's how we think, isn't it? So, we wear our knees out praying and praying for a sign. *But* have you ever considered this may not be the way God is operating?"

"When we look at the Bible, being in the will of God is

most often about *being* the people God created us to be. Most passages that deal with God's will tell us things like love God above all else, devote yourself to discipleship, become a person who exhibits the fruit of the Spirit. Jesus calls us to obedience to His Word. He will be happy with you whether you're in Alaska or Arizona as long as you love and serve Him."

Claire had never heard a sermon like this. Her secret fear had been she would choose the "wrong" job and end up out of God's will. She felt deeply grateful to Jake Weston for this sermon, and she decided to muster her courage and tell him so after church.

When the final invitation hymn had been sung, the congregation filed out of the sanctuary. Jake was standing at the door, shaking hands with all of the members as they went by. When Claire drew even with him, she stuck out her hand and opened her mouth to say how much the sermon had comforted her. Before any words came out, she was rendered completely mute. "Well, hello, Claire. I promise I won't run into you today."

Claire shut her mouth, opened it once more, found there were no words in it, and quickly shut it again.

Jake seemed unaffected by Claire's impression of a guppy. "I'm really sorry about plowing into you at the hospital that day. I recognized you when you came in today. I knew the Burkes had a granddaughter in nursing school, but I didn't realize it was you until this morning. Mrs. Lola Faye can't believe she didn't make the connections before, either.

Claire didn't know if this was a good thing or not.

Jake continued, "How're your classes going?"

"Fine, thanks," Claire stammered. She was completely appalled that he remembered their collision. Certain her neck was breaking out in hives, as it always did when she was embarrassed, Claire decided to skip her intended comments and flee. She was thinking only of getting to the white Buick and hiding her burning face when she heard someone behind her.

"Hi. I'm Sage Finley." It was the young mother, now holding one child precariously on her hip as the other girl raced round a nearby tree with a little boy in hot pursuit.

"I hope my girls weren't a distraction in church today. I

should've taken them in the nursery, but when I saw in the bulletin what the sermon would be about, I really wanted to hear it."

Claire relaxed a bit. Sage seemed to be genuinely interested in talking to her. She wasn't just going through the motions because Brother Weston had encouraged it.

"No, your girls were fine, really. They're so cute. What are their names?" Claire felt even better when she saw over Sage's shoulder that Jake Weston was busy mingling and didn't seem to notice her anymore.

"This is Matilda," she said as she hitched up the baby, who was trying desperately to escape. "No, Tillie, you can't get down. She likes to eat rocks." Sage pointed to her giggling older daughter, who had lured the little boy into yet another game of tag. "That's Magdalena but we call her Maggie."

"Is that your little boy?"

"Joshua? No, he belongs to our neighbor. She's homebound so we bring him to church with us. I'm glad you came to visit today. Hope you can come back."

Claire told her she was staying with her grandparents and would be coming to church with them all summer. Sage let out a delighted laugh that reminded Claire of a bell ringing. "Good! We're the next farm over from them. I'd love for you to visit sometime. Having two kids makes it a big hassle to get out and about, but we always like company coming over, don't we, Tillie?" Tillie squealed her agreement.

"It was nice to meet you, Sage." Claire said and found she actually meant it. "See you later," she called as Sage and the still wriggling Tillie went to gather Maggie, Joshua, and Mr. Finley.

Claire had just taken a step toward the car when she heard another voice calling her. It was light and whispery in a studied sort of way. Claire guessed immediately who it must be. She hoped she didn't wince outwardly as she turned to face the beautiful girl who was still calling, "Hello, hello."

Gliding over on her skyscraper heels, she gave Claire her most gorgeous smile and said, "So nice to see you here today. Jake always makes a point of recognizing visitors, so it's only proper I do the same. We have the reputation for being a friendly church and I'll certainly do my part to keep it that way."

Claire knew she ought to say thank you or offer some other pleasantry, but she was at a complete loss for how to respond to this woman. It was as though she were the self-appointed, public relations director for Dogwood Community Church. Claire found her hand being shaken with a delicate grip, although she felt the pressure of the French manicured fingernails a touch more than was necessary.

"I'm Miranda Davenport," she added in her faux, Marilyn Monroe voice. Miss Dogwood America now had a name.

Claire met Miranda's gaze and noticed that while her mouth was smiling, her eyes weren't. Their icy-blue stare washed over Claire, leaving her with the definite feeling she'd been weighed in the balance and found wanting.

"Nice to meet you. I'm Claire Burke."

"Yes, I know," Miranda replied. She didn't say anything else as she continued to look Claire up and down. "Cute shoes," she said, before she turned to go. She tossed her hair, and a quick "Have a nice afternoon," over her shoulder as she disappeared into the crowd.

When Claire finally crawled into the backseat of her grandparents' car, she sank down as low as she could without actually lying down. Miranda Davenport left such a bad taste in her mouth she was actually tempted to spit.

She knew she must avoid seeing Jake again. Claire didn't think it was healthy for a person to break out in hives on a regular basis. It was probably bad for the circulatory system. She'd have to look that up. Sage Finley had seemed nice, though and it had certainly been a good sermon. Truth be told, it had been an eventful Sunday morning.

As Gran and Paw slid into the front seat, Claire wondered if she'd ever be able to talk to Jake Weston without stammering and blushing. She kept her thoughts to herself as they rode in silence. The only sound was Gran's voice as she hummed a little tune. Gran seemed particularly pleased with herself. *What is she up to?*

When the Buick came to a halt in the dusty tire tracks that marked its home in the Burke's front yard, an old brown pickup truck slid in next to it. Claire was horrified to see Jake Weston piling out of the truck.

"Alright, Mrs. Millie, I'm ready for some of that good

cooking," Jake said.

"Well, you've come to the right place, Preacher," Gran replied. She gave Claire an annoyingly, triumphant smile as they all traipsed across the porch and into the little house.

Chapter Three

When Paw and Brother Jake had settled down to read the Sunday paper and discuss the state of the Union, Gran retreated to the kitchen to finish fixing dinner with Claire hot on her heels.

"That was a fine message this morning; don't you think, Claire?" Gran tied on her ragged apron as she said, "Fine preacher, that Brother Weston." She gave Claire a conspiratorial look. "A *very*, fine man, in general."

"Gran!" Claire hissed like an angry goose. "I hope you don't think I'm interested in Brother Jake." Using one of Gran's favorite phrases, Claire added, "Because if you do, you've got another think coming. I don't want to be involved with anyone right now. I might be halfway across the country in two months."

Gran looked up at Claire. Only five feet tall, Gran looked up at almost everyone. Her height, or lack thereof, and the twinkle in her blues eyes made her look positively impish as she said, "Why, Claire Elizabeth Burke, I have no idea what you're talkin' about. The church takes turns feedin' the preacher every Sunday. After all, he's a young, single fellow and it wouldn't be right for him to spend every Sunday afternoon all alone in the parsonage without a home-cooked meal, now would it?"

Claire eyed Gran suspiciously. Gran wasn't one to lie, but it seemed awfully convenient that this happened to be her week to host Jake Weston for lunch.

Gran continued. "Honey, you seem bound and determined that I'm trying to fix you up with this fine, young man, but I haven't said one, solitary word about it. Sure seems to be on your mind a lot, though. Reckon why that is?"

Before Claire could wipe the half-astonished, half-embarrassed expression from her face, she was handed a bowl of potatoes and a stick of butter. "Put this butter in the potatoes and mash 'em up," Gran instructed, closing down any chance to discuss Jake Weston. Claire didn't mind dropping the matter.

"How much do I add?" she asked.

"Whole stick."

"Good grief, Gran. Don't you want a little potato to go with your butter? All that saturated fat isn't good for your heart."

Gran was slicing freshly baked bread. She never looked up as she replied, "Claire, between my heart and my mouth, I'm gonna favor the mouth. You can't please all of the body all of the time."

They finished their dinner preparations in silence. Claire mashed the potatoes with more vigor than was necessary. *What in the world am I going to do with my hard-headed, bossy grandmother?* Gran clucked her tongue a few times. Claire chuckled as she considered that her grandmother was probably wondering the same thing about her granddaughter.

Gran poked her head into the living room and gave the familiar call of "Dinner!" Paw and Jake, still commiserating on the lack of rain in the area, came into the dining room.

The table was set with enough delicious food to make Claire almost forget the butterflies congregated in her stomach. Gran pointed her to the chair next to Jake.

"Claire, your grandmother makes the best pot roast of any lady in the church but you better keep what I think to yourself," he said with a smile and a wink in Gran's direction.

Gran looked pleased, Paw looked anxious to start eating, and Claire wasn't sure how she looked. But she did know Jake smelled like the woods after a rain and he had a dimple on his right cheek when he smiled.

"Preacher," Paw said in his gruff way, "why don't you ask the blessing?"

"Of course, Mr. Frank, I'd be happy to." Jake replied. "Do y'all join hands to pray?"

Claire shot Gran a pleading glance, but Gran completely ignored it, "Why, that would be just fine."

The first thing Claire noticed about Jake's hand was how rough it was. His grip was firm and somehow protective. It reminded Claire of how her daddy used to hold her hand when they crossed a busy street.

"Amen," Claire echoed a split second behind everyone else. She'd been trying to identify Jake's cologne and not listening to the prayer.

As pot roast, mashed potatoes, green beans, and bread were handed around the table, Claire began to relax. They ate heartily and washed it all down with Gran's sweet tea, a beverage more sugar than anything else. "That's good, stout tea," Paw said after a particularly satisfying, syrupy swig.

"Sweet tea. The only kind there is, in my book," Jake commented, helping himself to a slice of garden-fresh tomato. "Mr. Frank, my tomatoes aren't doing very well. I'm afraid that shower we had yesterday might be too little, too late. Do you think we'll be getting more rain any time soon? What's the weatherman been saying?"

"Unnnhh," Paw grunted through a mouthful of roast, "you can't listen to them. They ain't got a clue. Let's see, yesterday was the first of June. It rained a little, so that means it'll rain fifteen more days this month." Paw said this on authority of the Farmer's Almanac, which he believed in with almost religious fervor. He consulted it for everything, from planting and harvesting schedules to the best time for dehorning his cattle.

"I hope you're right. Would you like a tomato, Claire?"

Claire was so busy pondering the reliability of the Farmer's Almanac, she forgot to be bashful with Jake. "No, thank you," she said, her nose wrinkled with distaste.

"Not a big fan of tomatoes?" Jake asked, a bemused smile crinkling the corner of his hazel eyes.

"Fresh ones, no. It's a texture thing. Too slimy. Don't *even* get me started on boiled okra! But, I *do* like fried, green tomatoes and those little, bitty, cherry tomatoes that come on salads."

"Yeah, there are lots of kinds of tomatoes," Jake commented. "Probably more kinds of Baptists though."

Claire could tell he was waiting for her to ask what he meant, so she played along. "How so?"

"Well, there's Southern Baptists, Regular Baptists, General Baptists, Missionary Baptists, Primitive Baptists, Hard-Shell Baptists, Free-Will Baptists and even a few Foot-Washing Baptists scattered around. There's only one kind of Baptist you're not likely to find."

She took the bait again. "And what kind is that?"

"Unified Baptists. They're a terribly fractious lot. They love arguing and splitting almost as much as they love committees and pot-lucks." Jake punctuated his point with a shake of his head and a zealous bite of tomato.

"I grew up in a Baptist church," Claire commented, suppressing a smile and trying to appear very intent on buttering her bread.

"So did I, so I can talk. You know how it is. You can say what you want as long as it's about family. Oh, and if you really want to say something ugly, you've got to tack on a 'bless their hearts' at the end."

Claire looked at him in stunned silence but only for a moment before she saw Paw and Gran were laughing. Jake held her in a serious gaze for another second before he broke up, too.

"Well, I'm glad you have a sense of humor about church," Claire said. She'd never met a preacher quite like this one before.

"I've been through Seminary and I have a master's degree in Theology. You can't survive all that stuff without a sense of humor," Jake replied.

Without even realizing what was happening, Claire began chatting comfortably with Jake, as if they were old friends.

"What's your undergrad degree?"

"English," he replied, smiling at the slightly shocked expression on her face. "Literature, actually. I ain't never been no good at talking right, but I sure do like them purty books." Jake said this with such an exaggerated drawl, Claire laughed out loud and very nearly sent a mouthful of green beans into the air.

"I'm not a great orator, by any means. I don't like to break out the five-dollar words from the pulpit. I just like to share what's on my heart and try to get it across to the congregation in the clearest way possible without butchering the language too much. However I do love literature, novels, poetry, essays, you name it. Reading is one of my great loves."

Claire wondered what his other great loves were.

Paw chimed in, "Is college where you got the road poem by that Frost fellow? Jack Frost? No, that ain't right. Robert

Frost. That's it."

Jake seemed pleased. "I'm glad you remembered my illustration, Mr. Frank. Sometimes, a preacher wonders if he's being listened to at all. It's good to know somebody was awake out there today. Yes, I read 'The Road Not Taken' in a freshman English class. Our professor told us he believes it's one of the most misinterpreted poems of our time."

"Why is that?" Claire asked. "Isn't it about choosing the less traveled path and how that makes all the difference in your life?"

"Well, everyone thinks that's what Frost was saying. But if you read closely, the speaker in the poem tells you that both paths were really worn about the same. He may try to convince us he took the road less traveled, but he admits one was just as fair as the other."

"So, what's the point then?" Claire asked.

"I think it's saying the path isn't what makes the difference. It's what you do while you're on the path."

Jake began chewing the apple pie Gran had just brought out with great gusto, giving Claire an opportunity to sneak a sidelong glance at him. There was more to Jake Weston than his pretty eyes and dimples. He was the kind of man you could talk to about everything and nothing.

"Well," Claire began, unsure of what to say next.

"Now that's a deep subject," Jake replied seriously as he polished off the rest of the pie.

Claire had no idea what to make of this country preacher, but she decided she didn't mind spending time with him. *I will eat my shoe before I'll admit as much to Gran.*

Chapter Four

Once the dishes were cleared, Gran and Claire joined the men in the living room. They sat in companionable silence for a few moments before Gran exclaimed, "Oh, Brother Jake, you wouldn't happen to be going to visit Mrs. Lola Faye this afternoon, would you?" Gran knew the preacher spent his Sunday afternoons visiting church members who'd been sick or in the hospital.

"Yes, Ma'am. As a matter of fact, I'm heading that way when I leave here."

"Well, I'm not trying to run you off, but would you mind if I sent Claire with you to pick up my dishes? I plumb forgot them this morning after church." Gran, looking as innocent as a lamb, turned to Claire and said, "Would you mind doin' that for me, Sugar?"

The edges of Claire's mouth twitched in her effort to contain a laugh. Gran had to be the most obvious woman she'd ever met, but Claire was secretly happy to have another opportunity to talk with Brother Jake.

"I guess, Gran, if you *really* need them right now."

"Thank you, Sugar. You're so sweet," Gran said before burying her face in the newspaper. Paw, who had already drifted off for his Sunday afternoon nap, let out a snore.

Jake took the hint. "Well, Claire, if you're ready, I guess we can head over to Mrs. Lola Faye's. She told me this morning after church you'd been her nurse. I'm sure she'd be glad to see you again."

Jake said his goodbyes to Gran, complimented the meal for the tenth time, and headed out the door. Claire followed him, glancing over her shoulder at Gran, who was reading *Garfield* as if it were the most fascinating thing she'd ever run across.

They passed quickly under the screeching mockingbirds. When Claire climbed into Jake's truck, she plastered herself against the door. After all, she was a young, single person and so was he. Small towns could stir up more dirt than a summer dust-storm.

"How far is it to Mrs. Nugent's?" Suddenly, being alone with the preacher was making the pot roast do somersaults in her stomach.

"Only about ten miles," he said. "So, I hear you're going to be graduating from nursing school soon. I bet you'll be glad to get out and find a job. Planning to leave the state?"

Claire would've answered the same question in the affirmative without a moment's thought only a week ago. But now, she hesitated for a split second. "That's the plan. I'm going to talk with my advisor next week when I take my finals. We're pretty good friends and she said she'd use her connections to see what she could find for me."

"Are you looking at any place in particular?" Jake asked as they bounced along the highway.

Claire stared out at the wild day-lilies and buttercups in the ditches. Beyond them in an open field, rolls of golden, sweet smelling hay dried in the midday sun.

"Atlanta, maybe. Dallas might be alright. I'll just have to wait and see." Claire hoped Jake wouldn't ask her why she didn't stay here, because she was suddenly unsure of what answer she would give.

Luckily, Jake didn't press the subject but the one he chose next wasn't her favorite topic of discussion either.

"Well, I'm sure your mom and dad are proud of you."

When Claire didn't reply immediately, Jake looked over at her. She was twisting and untwisting the skirt fabric on her lap.

"Did I say something to upset you, Claire?"

"No, it's fine. My dad is very proud of me. He's been telling me to make something of myself since I can remember. I'm sure Momma would be pleased. She's the one who first told me I'd make a good nurse. She died of cancer when I was eight."

In her mind, Claire was six years old again, holding her mother's hand, looking down through a hospital glass at the wrinkled, pink newborn baby of a family friend. She remembered watching as nurses tended to the other infants, all of whom were wearing knits caps and sleeping off the fatigue of the strange journey they'd just made.

"Momma, who are those ladies in there with the

babies?"

"Those are the nurses, Claire. Nurses take care of people who can't take care of themselves. Like babies. Or sick people. They help people."

Her mother had twirled one of her auburn pigtails, a habit of hers when she and Claire were talking, and said, "A nurse should have a caring heart. You'd make a wonderful nurse one day, Claire Bear."

She was jolted from her reverie by the awareness of Jake watching her. Claire hadn't realized she was twining a lock of hair around and around her fingers, forming it into a glossy ringlet before letting it go and starting the process again.

"I'm so sorry, Claire," he said simply, turning back to his driving.

"Thank you, Brother Jake. I don't talk about Momma much." Claire remembered how she used to feel like she was being tied in a knot on the inside when she mentioned her mother. Now, she could recall the happy times with a smile and without feeling the resonating pain of loss ringing through her body. "You wouldn't believe some of the things people say, trying to be helpful."

"Like what?" Jake asked softly.

"Well, like…you loved your mother, but God loved her more so He took her home to be with Him." Claire remembered a gentle, grandfatherly preacher bending over and telling her that with a kind pat on the shoulder.

"I hope I don't sound rude, but why would anyone say something so dumb? That makes God sound like He's a big bully who takes away what you love most just because He wanted it for Himself. I don't think He works that way. Do you?"

Claire smiled, relieved he'd been brave enough to say what she'd been thinking. "No, I don't."

Jake looked thoughtful. He scratched his chin, his fingers making a rasping sound as they scraped across the stubble. "I think I should preach about this. How God suffers with us and hurts when His children are in pain. Would you mind if I did that, Claire?"

"I guess I've inspired you, huh?"

They were turning into the gravel driveway that led to Mrs. Lola Faye's trailer house. This time, Jake kept his eyes fixed straight ahead as he replied, "You certainly have."

****

Mrs. Lola Faye Nugent's house seemed to serve only as a backdrop for the flowers covering the yard, the porch, and anything else that would stand still, with riotous blooms. Hydrangeas in shades of blue and purple formed a border around the trailer. Mimosa trees, their blossoms like giant, pink powder-puffs, competed for attention with frilly, crepe myrtle bushes, some of which had grown so tall they shaded the yard like trees. A rose bed showed off along the sidewalk, while sunflowers and shocking pink hibiscus joined in the celebration of color run amok. Boxwood shrubs and Nandinas tried to sober their more colorful neighbors, but were fighting a losing battle. Vivid impatiens edged in among them, urging them to brighten up and join in the blossoming festivities.

"Wow!" Claire said appreciatively as they picked their way through the multitude of flower beds and climbed the wooden front steps, ducking to avoid hanging baskets of petunias in the process. "Look at this yard! I can't imagine having so many flowers to take care of."

"Don't have a green thumb, huh?" Jake said as he rang the doorbell, which sounded the notes of "You Are My Sunshine" throughout the house.

"I have the 'Black Thumb of Death'. I could probably kill petrified wood."

Mrs. Nugent peeked through the white muslin curtains, gave a little start, and opened the door. "Well, land's sakes! What are you doing here, Claire? Brother Jake's never brought company before when he's come to visit." She said this as if it were a very significant piece of information and peered at the two of them over her reading glasses.

Claire took note of that interesting, little tidbit and tucked it away to chew on later. "It is so good to see you again, Mrs. Nugent."

"Dear, we aren't in that hospital anymore. I'm Mrs. Lola Faye around here."

"I came to get Gran's dishes and to see how you're doing. The whole time you were in the hospital, talking about your church and your friends, I never realized you lived so close to my grandparents. You're right down the road from where I spent most of my summers."

Mrs. Lola Faye motioned them both inside her tiny

living room. "Well, I didn't always live here. When my Bud was living, we farmed a big hundred acre tract over by the river. He always said, 'Now Lola Faye, when I've bought the farm, you sell *this* farm and live off the money.'"

Mrs. Lola Faye laughed at the remembrance of her husband's joke, which Claire found a touch morbid, before continuing, "So, that's what I did. Got enough out of the deal to buy this tin box, put a little in the bank, and start plantin' flowers. I always said when I was an old widder lady, I'd have some flower beds. While we were farming, I never had much time for that. Now, all I've got is time."

The jovial tone of her voice faltered and a hint of wistfulness crept in. "Well, I've done it up right, don't you think? The gardens are a little shabby right now, owing to me being in the hospital, but I'm gettin' them back in shape."

"They're beautiful, Mrs. Lola Faye. Everybody in the county knows you've got the prettiest yard around," Jake said. She didn't try to deny it and seemed happy to hear him say so.

While Mrs. Lola Faye went to fix lemonade for her visitors, Claire studied the pictures that lined the walls. A faded portrait of a young Lola Faye, her hair in an astonishingly, high bouffant style, and a sturdy looking man with dark hair and eyes, smiled down at her. *That must be Bud.*

Scattered around the room were more pictures, all of a boy with white-blonde hair and startling green eyes. Claire's gaze traveled across the timeline of a life displayed in the small living room. The pictures started next to the front door with a chubby-faced baby, progressing to a gap-toothed little boy over the mantle, a somewhat sullen adolescent by the kitchen door, and finally to a handsome young man in a cap and gown directly over Mrs. Lola Faye's rocking chair. The graduation picture seemed to be the most recent, although it appeared to be quite a few years old.

"That's my boy, Jesse." Mrs. Lola Faye returned trying to carry the lemonades and get along without her walker. Jake gently guided her to the nearest armchair and handed Claire a drink before taking the other for himself.

Claire noticed a small snapshot on the wooden, end table beside the couch. "Is this him, too?" The picture showed a man of about thirty, sporting a thick beard, and standing in front of a tiny log cabin.

"Yes, that's the latest one he sent. He's living up in the northern part of the state. Built that house himself while working for a logger up there. Always been a bit of a wanderer, that boy. He was even a ranch hand in Montana for a while."

Mrs. Lola Faye's eyes took on a distant, almost pained expression, when she mentioned Montana. For a moment, it appeared she'd forgotten Claire and Jake were there. She glanced up with a small, apologetic smile and continued.

"He's had some rough patches, but he's doing good now. Calls and writes all the time. I'm so glad he's back in Arkansas. It makes me feel better, knowing he's not too awful far away, even if he doesn't get down this way much. Just so happy he's back." She grew quiet, looked out the window at a swaying dogwood tree, and smiled to herself.

The way she touched the picture of her happy, beaming son, as if it were somehow sacred, spoke volumes. Claire surmised there had been a time when Mrs. Lola Faye didn't know if she'd ever have any new pictures to add to her collection. When she talked about Jesse being back, she didn't mean just back in the state. Wherever he'd journeyed, his mother had worried he'd never return.

Glancing at Jake for a clue on how to proceed with the conversation, Claire noticed he didn't look surprised by Mrs. Lola Faye slipping into silent reverie. *He knows the story of whatever Jesse did during his 'rough patches.' I guess that makes sense. She probably didn't have anyone else to talk to except her pastor. She did say he'd been like family to her.*

Claire felt like an outsider who'd stepped into a private conversation, although no one was speaking. Finally, Jake asked how Mrs. Lola Faye's hip was healing.

"Well, I'm fine as frog's hair. Should be off this walker pretty soon. I can tell you one thing, I ain't gonna be mopping no more. If I can't stand on a soapy floor without falling and breaking something, then I'll just have nasty floors."

Claire knew if Mrs. Lola Faye was at all like Gran, the prospect of having *anything* dirty in her home was horrifying. Claire heard herself say, "Mrs. Lola Faye, why don't you let me come over and mop for you while I'm down for the summer? I could do it once a week or so. How about that?"

She'd had no intention of being someone's unpaid maid during her time off from school, but something about Mrs. Lola Faye's predicament moved her. What if it were Gran without anyone nearby to talk to or help her in the house? She was just as surprised to make the offer as she was to hear Mrs. Lola Faye accept it.

"Oh, that would be wonderful. You're the sweetest girl, just like Millie. She'd bend over backwards for any of her neighbors."

They decided Wednesday would be Claire's first cleaning visit as she and Jake left with Gran's dishes in tow. They wove their way through the maze of blooms and climbed back into Jake's, dusty, brown Chevy.

"That was really nice of you to offer to clean for Mrs. Lola Faye," Jake said as they jostled along the potholed highway.

"Yeah, well, I'm usually pretty self-centered. Don't know what came over me." Claire replied, only half joking.

"It's just Dogwood. Everybody helps everybody else. Guess it just rubs off on you."

When they rolled to a stop under the mockingbird-laden trees, Claire scrambled out, precariously balancing Gran's dishes. "Well, I'll see you next Sunday, Brother Jake."

"Have a good week, Claire." He hesitated, as if there were something more he wanted to say. "Um, good luck on your tests."

"Thanks. You have a good week, too."

She made her way slowly up the sidewalk. She was a bit annoyed with herself when she realized she was hoping he might call her back. She really hated to admit how sorely disappointed she was when the engine rumbled to life and he headed down the highway.

Good thing Gran needed this CorningWare back so desperately.

"Gran, I brought your dishes back," Claire called. "Where do you want them?"

"Oh, just put them up in the cabinet over the refrigerator. Push them all the way to the back, Sugar, I hardly ever use them." Gran yelled back, a definite note of triumph in her voice.

Chapter Five

Monday was beauty shop day for Gran. Since Claire could remember, Gran had worn her hair in a little helmet of fluffy, white curls that resembled a French poodle. It had grown thinner and shrunk a bit over the years, but the basic style remained the same, as did the routine. Once a week, Gran drove into Pickens and visited Lottie's Beauty Box to have her hair rolled and set. She would have it shampooed, wound tightly around little pink curlers, and then dried under a big bonnet dryer. Lottie would pick it out into the proper spherical shape, spray it with enough hairspray to make another hole in the ozone layer and Gran would be set for the week.

When they arrived in Pickens, Claire was once again struck by how small the town was. A tiny discount store, a fast food restaurant, and a bank were the main businesses, although there were smaller ones lining the square around the courthouse. Claire stopped at the only red light, turned right, and pulled up in front of the block that housed Lottie's Beauty Box.

The overwhelming smell of a perm in progress greeted them as they stepped inside. A lady of about fifty was busily applying chemicals to the head of a client who seemed to be sleeping. Claire wondered if she had passed out from the fumes.

"Hey there, Millie. I'll be done with Mrs. Shepherd in just a minute." As she talked, Lottie never stopped working. She'd obviously been in the hair business for a very long time.

"Mrs. Sheppard, MRS. SHEPPARD!" Lottie's client mumbled something about potato salad, opened her eyes, and looked surprised to find herself in the beauty shop. Lottie escorted her to the dryer and sat her down underneath the hood. The dryer's steady roar had the narcoleptic lady back asleep in no time.

31

After Gran climbed in the chair, Lottie had to pump the pedal and raise it several inches to reach Gran's head. The noise of Mrs. Sheppard's dryer made it impossible to talk without shouting. Claire wasn't very interested in thumbing through out-of-date issues of *Good Housekeeping*.

"GRAN, I'M GOING FOR A WALK!"

"OK! BE DONE IN ABOUT THIRTY MINUTES!" Gran hollered back.

Lottie smiled, a comb between her teeth, and waved as Claire opened the pink front door and stepped out onto the sunny sidewalk.

Lottie's Beauty Box shared a block with an abstract and title office, a discount flooring store, and an exterminator business called "The Termite-inators". None of those looked very intriguing. Claire crossed the narrow side street and stepped onto the awning-shaded walk of the next block.

The first business she came to was Feel The Burn Gym and Tanning Salon. Claire had always held a certain amount of disdain for those who tanned themselves to an unnatural orange shade, but her curiosity began to get the better of her. Just a little touch of color would be nice,

She stood debating for a minute longer, then stepped into the building. A chipper voice called out, "Hey, there! Welcome to Feel The Burn."

Claire saw a thickset woman in her late forties busily doing abdominal crunches on the floor of the foyer. She bounced to her feet, her long, gray ponytail swishing from side to side, as she approached.

"I'm Dixie Winkle. What can I do for you today?" Her rather chunky build didn't fit Claire's impression of a personal trainer, although the certificate behind the front desk declared her to be one.

"Um," Claire hesitated, "I think I might like to try tanning. I...I mean...I've never tanned before."

Dixie sprang at her with disconcerting speed. She grabbed Claire by the wrist, lifted her arm high in the air, and examined it from every angle with the air of someone selecting a cut of beef at the butcher shop.

"Do you freckle?" Dixie asked seriously.

"Uh...yes, I do.

"Burn easily, I imagine?"

"Yes, Ma'am."

"Just as I suspected. You're a redhead, too, and that makes our job more difficult. Still, it can be done. I'm a professional and there's not a woman on earth I can't get to a deep, tropical tan if you've got enough patience."

Claire was beginning to regret coming in at all and was trying to think of a way to excuse herself. All the while, Dixie was bouncing down a hallway with Claire's wrist still firmly in her grasp. "Now, since this is your first time, I'll let you tan for free. It's a complimentary session I do for new clients."

Claire was ushered into a tiny, hot room. A tanning bed, bright with a bluish light, stood before her. It looked exactly like a glowing coffin.

Dixie was still prattling on, but Claire wasn't listening. She was looking across the hall into the next room. There, on a stair machine, glistening with sweat and yet somehow still wearing a full face of makeup, was Miranda Davenport.

"You'll need five minutes is my guess, maybe six, but we'll see what you get with five. Wear these goggles, remember to change your position every sixty seconds and just push 'Start' when you're ready. I'll check on you when your time's up."

Dixie must have noticed the somewhat unpleasant look on Claire's face and misinterpreted its cause. She stopped chattering and said, "Don't worry, you'll be fine. I was nervous my first time, too. Thought Jesus would return and I'd be left behind cause I was being vain and wicked, lying in the tanning bed, thinking about my appearance." Dixie laughed heartily. "Ah, but that was when I was young and silly. You have fun." She bounded out of the room, shutting the door and blocking Claire's view of Miranda.

How am I going to get out of here without being seen? She wasn't in the mood to talk to Miranda. Or more likely, to be *talked at* by Miranda.

As Claire stood debating how best to deal with this dilemma, she absentmindedly pushed the 'Start' button and was startled at the loud whirring noise of the bed. It sounded like a giant microwave. Between the noise of the bed and the blaring radio Dixie had going in the exercise room, she could probably sneak quietly out and make a dash back to Lottie's without being seen.

Opening the door a crack, she peeked across the hall.

Dixie was nowhere to be seen, and Miranda was apparently absorbed in firming her thighs. She never looked up from her leg lifts.

Claire stuck a toe out into the hall, glanced quickly in both directions, then scurried back towards the front door.

Just as her hand touched the knob, Dixie popped up from behind the front desk where she'd been hidden from Claire's view, doing pushups.

"Done already? Let me see you?"

Claire sheepishly let Dixie examine her arm. "I didn't really...I mean...I decided...it's just..." she stammered, but Dixie shushed her.

"Well, I guess I didn't properly prepare you. I should've told you to put on some accelerator lotion. And I need to warn you, you absolutely can not take a shower within the next six hours." Dixie looked at Claire gravely and added, "If you do, you'll wash your tan off."

Claire didn't even bother to ask how that could be. Checking over her shoulder to make sure Miranda wasn't coming down the hall, Claire nodded mutely at Dixie.

"Now, before you come in to tan again, you need to make sure you really ex-fuh-late yourself well." Trying to look deeply impressed by this new information, Claire pushed the door open and took a half-step onto the sidewalk.

"Ex-fuh-lating is the secret." Dixie continued. "Not many people realize this," she said in hushed tones as she leaned towards Claire, "but there is an *art* to tanning." She fell silent and nodded seriously, as if she'd just revealed the secret of turning lead into gold.

Claire seized the opportunity. "I'm sure there is. Thank you so much for your time."

She made a hasty exit onto the sidewalk and was halfway to the end of the block when she heard a familiar, airy voice calling her name, "Claire? Is that you?"

Other than feigning a sudden attack of deafness, Claire saw no way of ignoring the rapidly approaching Miranda without being terribly rude. She made a face, just to get it out of her system, then tried to look pleasant and turned to meet her.

"Hello, Miranda," Claire said.

Miranda stopped a few feet in front of where Claire was standing, tossed her gym bag into the seat of a candy-apple red convertible and said, breathlessly, "Ahh, there's nothing like a good workout." She looked at Claire's long, thin arms and added in a voice so sweet it could've caused cavities, "You really should try Dixie's new upper body machine. It adds definition and builds muscle, takes care of scarecrow arms." She laughed a delicate, mirthless laugh and continued in the same saccharine voice. "I come here on my lunch break and work out. How about you? What brings you to 'Feel The Burn'?"

Claire muttered something about how she'd thought of trying the tanning bed, but changed her mind. She wanted to think she was being overly sensitive, that Miranda didn't have it out for her and was really just a very sweet girl. *Maybe, if I tried to have a real conversation with her?*

"So, where do you work?"

Miranda pointed across the square to a building with a red and white striped awning emblazoned with the words *Buzby Family Dentistry.*

"Dr. Buzby is a dear, dear friend of the family. He has trouble keeping dental hygienists. I mean, after all, dental professionals aren't just flocking to Pickens looking for jobs," she said. "So, I took the job to help him out. "

"Oh, that's nice,"

Claire's succinct reply didn't seem to strike Miranda as an appropriate acknowledgment of the noble self-sacrifice she'd made.

"I could get a job anywhere, practically. Dental hygienists are very much in demand. In fact, I was offered a job in Orlando just last week. But, of course, I turned it down." She looked at Claire as if she should know what she was implying.

"I guess you don't have very far to drive to work," Claire ventured. Oh, she dearly hoped Miranda would have to be back at work shortly.

"Oh, I don't *live* in Pickens," Miranda replied, as if Claire had suggested she lived in a barn. "I commute from Aberdeen." When Claire's blank expression betrayed her ignorance of where or what Aberdeen might be, Miranda continued. "It's a very nice gated community in Bryant, about thirty minutes from here. I really don't mind the drive. After all, I come down six days a week. Monday through Friday for work, and then Sunday for church."

She tilted her head to the side and inquired, "What did you think of Jake's sermon on Sunday?" Miranda waited for Claire's response, one perfectly arched eyebrow raised skyward.

"I thought it was very insightful, and honest, too." Claire chose her words carefully, not wanting to give Miranda any inkling of how much she'd come to admire Jake during their time together on Sunday afternoon.

Miranda narrowed her eyes for a split second, scrutinizing Claire's face. Then she flashed her glow-in-the dark smile, the product of quite a few whitening treatments at Dr. Buzby's. *She's had so much bleach in her mouth, I bet her breath smells like Clorox.* Claire gave her a faint smile in return.

"I think Jake's a wonderful man, in the pulpit and out." Miranda tossed off the last phrase as if she'd spent countless hours with him. "The very first time we met, he helped me get my car started." She gave the red Mustang a loving pat. "He had taken a group of ladies from the church to the Magnolia Springs Botanical Gardens. I was presiding over their annual flower show as one of my duties as Miss Magnolia Springs," Miranda said, modestly.

Claire merely nodded. Apparently, Miranda had expected Claire to be awed or surprised at learning she was talking to pageant royalty. Miranda fit the stereotype of a beauty queen to a tee. It would've been like asking Claire to be shocked that the Pope was Catholic.

Ignoring the unenthusiastic response, Miranda continued. "I was having trouble getting my car started. Sally can be quite a pill sometimes," she said, gesturing toward the car with an affected giggle. "Anyway, I asked Jake for help and he got her started just like that," Miranda said with a snap of her perfectly sculpted nails. "Of course, we got to talking and I asked what he did for a living. He invited me to visit his church, so naturally, I took him up on the offer. I've been going to church there ever since.

Claire had had enough of this fascinating little discussion. "I have to get back to Lottie's and take Gran home. Nice seeing you, Miranda. Have a nice day."

"I'll see you at church," said Miranda, giving Claire a sweeping glance. "Don't give up on tanning just yet," she said as she propped one perfectly bronzed leg up on her car and pretended to tie an already tied shoelace. "It just takes longer to get results when a person is, well, pale to begin with." She smiled benignly, slid into her sparkling sports car and drove away.

Claire stood staring after her. Obviously, her chat with Miranda wasn't going to be the start of a beautiful friendship. In fact, Claire decided if she didn't want her dislike for Miranda to grow into downright hatred, she'd better just steer clear of Miss Dogwood America altogether.

Turning back toward Lottie's, Claire saw Gran step onto the sidewalk. Her hair was a perfect cloud of sudsy-looking white curls. Claire hurried towards her, trying to shake the nagging concern that Miranda's fascination with Jake wasn't one sided. She'd never seen anything from him to confirm it, but then again she didn't know him that well. She had to remind herself that none of this mattered because she wasn't going to be here much longer anyway.

As they drove back to Dogwood in silence, Claire renewed her vow to start applying for nursing jobs as soon as her tests were over. That was the plan she'd made long ago, and that was the plan she'd stick to.

"I hope you weren't too bored waiting for me, Claire," Gran said at last.

"No, I had an eventful afternoon," Claire replied. She told Gran about meeting Dixie Winkle, but left out her run-in with Miranda Davenport.

"Sugar, that Dixie Winkle is as crazy as a road lizard. You stay out of them tanning beds cause they'll fry your innards like an egg."

With that, they pulled into the yard of the little, white house. Claire promised to leave her internal organs uncooked, and Gran went in to start supper, leaving her alone on the porch swing, swinging just as high and fast as a porch swing could. *I'll try my best to stay away from Miranda Davenport, too.*

Chapter Six

Claire finished her tests and headed down the familiar halls of St. Bernadette's Medical Education Center, nose buried in notes for the post-test ritual of trying to figure out how many questions she'd answered wrong. She wondered whether she'd remembered the correct dosages for treating seizures in adults. What was the name of that medicine used for anxiety attacks? Had she written it was prescribed for acne instead?

Claire rounded a corner and stepped into the suite that housed the faculty offices. A gold nameplate on the first door read "Rita Sparks, Professor of Nursing." The familiar, brisk voice responded with a sharp "Enter!"

Rita was marking papers and muttering something about "disturbing incompetence and ignorance." She glanced up at Claire and her narrow, angular face split into a wide grin.

"Claire! I'm so glad you came by. I was just grading some first-year students' work." Rita took off her glasses and rubbed her temples, "It's good to be reminded that we do have a few bright students at this school, after all"

"I'm sure it's not that bad, Professor Sparks," Claire remarked. She'd always thought Rita a bit overly dramatic when it came to bemoaning the academic prospects of her pupils. "I came to see if you had any leads for me. We talked about it last month, remember?"

Rita Sparks began quickly shuffling through a pile of papers. "Today, one of the best second years we had told me she was pregnant and putting her nursing career on hold to be a 'stay-at-home-mom.'" She made quotation marks in the air with her fingers as she said the last phrase, then ran her fingers through her cropped hair in dismay. "She was such a brilliant girl." Rita continued shaking her head and rummaging around for something on her desk. "Ah, here it is!"

Claire reached out and took the sheet of paper Rita thrust toward her. "I hunted down an old friend of mine who's the Nurse Recruiter at Dallas Presbyterian Hospital. I put in a good word for you," she said with a meaningful nod. "I've got an excellent feeling about this, Claire. I told him what a go-getter you are and how you're really going to make something of yourself. If I were you, I'd fax a resume as soon as possible. My machine's on the blink or you could do it right now. Well, I hate to run, but I've got another test to give. Keep me posted."

Rita Sparks swept out of the office, leaving Claire staring down at the sheet of paper in her hands. She decided she'd go visit her father, stay for supper, and use his fax machine to send her resume off that night.

Dallas, Claire walked slowly back to her car. It really wasn't *that* far from home.

She realized with a slight pang that, when she thought of home, images of Dogwood came to mind. She'd been to Dallas with her father several times for business trips. All she'd seen of it were the high rises and office buildings visible from their hotel window. It all seemed concrete gray in her memory, so different from the faded red porch swing and sun warmed, golden hayfields of the Burke farm.

I'm sure I can make myself at home there. I'll just have to learn my way around and get used to it, that's all, Claire admonished herself as she sped along toward the home of F. Monroe Burke, Jr.

****

Claire's Camry slid to a stop in front of the massive three-story, brick house her father called home when he wasn't sleeping at the office or dining with clients. She fumbled for her key as she walked between perfectly symmetrical shrubs that bordered the walkway. The lawn service had certainly been earning its pay. Landscape lights illuminated a lawn so immaculately groomed it might have been artificial.

She pushed open the heavy oak door and listened to her steps echoing in the cavernous entryway. The vaulted ceilings caught her words and flung them back to her. "Dad? Where are you?"

Her father's sonorous, bass voice resonated through the house. "I'm in the formal dining room, Claire."

She found her father sitting alone at the long, highly polished, mahogany dining room table. His suit jacket was tossed over the chair next to him, a silk tie hung loosely around his neck, and his white shirt sleeves were rolled up. Monroe Burke looked relaxed and pleased with himself as he sipped a drink and smiled at his daughter.

"Frieda's really outdone herself tonight. Best decision I ever made, hiring a cook. Try this Beef Wellington. It's superb!" he boomed at Claire as she sat down across from him.

"Well, you're certainly in a good mood," Claire noted as Frieda slipped in silently, set a plate before her, and vanished back into the kitchen just as quietly. "Thank you," Claire called to her retreating figure, before turning back to her father, who was swirling his beverage around in a goblet and surveying the room with great satisfaction.

"I just won a lawsuit for a big client. Violated a non-compete clause and...it's all lawyer talk. I won't bore you with the details but it was a decisive victory." Monroe took a drink and set the glass down triumphantly. "So, how's my little country bumpkin doing?"

Claire frowned. Her father could never pass up an opportunity to rib her about her affection for "the boonies." He viewed it as a sort of childish attachment Claire should've outgrown by now and was both amused and concerned she hadn't.

"I'm fine, Daddy. Gran and Paw are good, too, in case you were wondering," Claire added.

Monroe furrowed his dark brows, leveled his most intimidating stare at his daughter and, brandishing a butter knife for emphasis, said, "You are unaware of this crucial fact; I spoke with both my parents this morning after you'd left for the day. I am abreast of the news from Dogwood, such as it is, and would thank you not to insinuate I have been a negligent son. Your implied accusation was made without full knowledge of all relevant evidence."

Claire chewed her roll thoughtfully, then said, "You haven't lost your touch. All these years out of the prosecutor's office and you still make a great closing argument. Even if you do sound more like a defense attorney at the moment."

Her father's chiseled face lit up with a self-satisfied

smile, "I'll take that as a compliment. The closing argument part, not the defense attorney bit."

Claire watched him for a moment. "Daddy, why did you leave the D. A.'s office? Mom always talked about how you loved your job."

"Bigger and better things, Claire," said Monroe, fiddling with his silverware. He looked around the gleaming room, richly furnished and decorated with the finest art money could buy. "I couldn't have had all this if I'd stayed where I was. It was a good job, sure. I loved it, but it was just a stepping stone." He paused, reviewed what he'd just said in his mind, decided it was a satisfactory explanation, and nodded slightly to himself.

He looked uncomfortable as he met Claire's questioning eyes.

"Speaking of first jobs, what's going on with your prospects? Rita Sparks dug up anything for you yet?"

"Actually, that's why I'm here. I need to fax my resume to Dallas Presbyterian Hospital. Rita put in a good word for me with the Nurse Recruiter. She really thinks I've got a shot at being hired there." She moved the food around her plate aimlessly and waited for Monroe's response.

"That's wonderful news, Claire! Dallas is a great city. So much to do and see. Lots to keep you busy. The hospital has a good reputation in the medical community, if I'm not mistaken, and should be a good starting point for you. You know, if you'd take my suggestion and become a nurse practitioner, you'd make more money and no one ever said you couldn't become a doctor. Now there's some money in that, especially if you specialize. Of course, the malpractice insurance is astronomical."

He went on for a few minutes before he realized Claire wasn't listening. She was chewing her bottom lip and looking absently at the table.

"What's the matter, Claire?" he demanded. "This is very exciting. It's what you've always wanted, yet you're acting as though someone's just sentenced you to life in prison." He snorted, just like Paw did when he was frustrated with a wayward cow, then went back to his Beef Wellington.

Claire finished her meal quickly, gathered her resume papers from her room, and went to her father's office. She dialed the fax number, slipped the papers in, and pressed the button. She shuddered a bit as the machine made a soft whirring sound and the papers were pulled through.

It was done. When Jasper Johnson arrived in his office the next morning, he'd find the impressive resume of a very bright girl just waiting for her chance to get out of Arkansas.

Isn't that what I'm waiting for? The nagging headache she'd had for most of the day started to pound insistently.

"Dad, I'm heading back home, I mean, to Dogwood."

Monroe followed her to the front door, looking very pleased with himself, his world, and his up-and-coming daughter.

"Drive safely, Claire Bear." He gave her a bear hug and kissed her hair. Pausing, he looked into her bright green eyes. "You look so much like Sherry. She'd be so proud of you."

The sun was slowly descending behind the pine trees when she arrived in Dogwood. A heavy, silver mist floated across Paw's hayfield, making its way to the little, white house, ready to wrap it up for another night's rest.

The mockingbirds sang their final song of the day. Claire started to open the front door, then let it scrape to a stop, and held it halfway open. She turned and looked up at the mockingbirds. They were warbling their hearts out, trying their best to sound like field larks, or brown thrushes, or bobwhites. She suddenly felt very tired and went wearily into the house.

Chapter Seven

Claire arrived at Mrs. Lola Faye's the next day bearing zucchini bread. Paw had been overly zealous with his zucchini planting and now, Gran proclaimed, they were "plum covered up in the things." Gran was trying her best to use them all before they ruined. It was against her nature to let anything go to waste. She'd even resorted to placing them in people's cars at church if they were careless enough to leave their doors unlocked.

Mrs. Lola Faye, still using a walker to get around, showed Claire where the cleaning supplies were and thanked her profusely for being such a sweetheart.

"I'm glad to help." She'd spent a restless night, thinking in circles about jobs and Dallas and moving. At last, she'd dropped into a fitful sleep, the kind that comes suddenly upon those who are too tense for sweet, heavy-eyed drifting. For the rest of the night, she'd alternated between short bursts of sleep and sudden wakefulness. It was true what Gran always told her. A weary body may rest, but there's no rest for a weary mind. Claire was glad to have something, anything, to occupy her day besides her own thoughts.

She slopped soapy water on the linoleum and began her task with vigor. Mrs. Lola Faye insisted on puttering around, straightening and tidying the already neat rooms as she went. Since mopping such a small home took very little time, Claire offered to dust before she left. The idea of Mrs. Lola Faye tottering on a chair, reaching as high as she could to dust bookshelves and knick-knacks sent shivers down Claire's spine.

"That'll be fine, Honey, on one condition. You've got to stay for supper."

"I'd love to stay, Mrs. Lola Faye," Claire replied, busily dusting the pictures of Jesse Nugent. Her hair had escaped from under the bandana she'd used to tame it and there were streaks of dirt across her nose. She'd worked up quite a sweat from mopping. Mrs. Lola Faye kept her thermostat set very high to save on electricity bills, and the trailer was uncomfortably warm in the June heat.

"Claire, you need to sit down. You're all red in the face. Land's sakes, child! Have a drink before you pass out," Mrs. Lola Faye ordered. Since she was thirsty and also on the verge of a sneezing fit from breathing in all the dust, Claire complied and joined Mrs. Lola Faye in the kitchen. She was still carrying her dust rag and the picture of Jesse standing on the porch of his log cabin.

Mrs. Lola Faye handed Claire a tin cup full of icy water, then fixed one for herself. As they sat sipping their water and discussing whether this summer was hotter than the last, Mrs. Lola Faye's eyes fell on the picture in Claire's hand.

"He's looking more and more like his daddy," she said. A faded smile touched her lips and her eyes wandered around the trailer. "When me and Bud married, we were so poor, we only had one kitchen chair. So I sat in his lap while we ate. Always said we'd have to get some more chairs when the babies came. But they never came. Twenty four years, it was just me and him. Working, waiting, hoping. Finally, we stopped hoping." The long ago emptiness echoed in the hollow tone of her voice. Claire thought how it must have been to ache for a child for so many years. More years than Claire had even been alive.

Mrs. Lola Faye's eyes brightened and an expression of tenderness relaxed her face. "Then Jesse came along. I always said I should've named him Isaac, 'cause when that doctor told me I didn't have nothing wrong with me nine months wouldn't cure, I just laughed in his face. When I finally believed it was true, I was half out of my mind with joy. And Bud! Oh, when he held that little boy, I thought he was going to bust at the seams. He'd smile so wide and puff his chest out like a bullfrog. Called Jesse 'Son' all the time, just 'cause he was so proud to have one. He was Jesse's hero, I can tell you that much. Maybe more. I'd almost say Jesse idolized his daddy. Kindly worshipped him, I reckon."

Her wrinkled brow knitted together and her usually loud voice dropped to an almost inaudible whisper. "When Bud died, it happened real sudden. Had a stroke one day out in the field. I always thanked the Lord he didn't linger, crippled or whatnot. Bud wouldn't have wanted that. It was the best way to go, really, quick, no long illness or nothing like that. But Jesse," She stopped, looked at Claire for the first time.

Claire realized Mrs. Lola Faye needed to tell this story. "He wasn't prepared, was he? I mean, Jesse wasn't prepared to lose his dad."

Mrs. Lola Faye shook her head. "He was away working in Montana when it happened. When he came home for the funeral, he just walked for days. He must've walked the farm a thousand times, not sayin' nothin'. Just walkin'. He kept his eyes on the ground and went as fast as he could up and down the fencerows. He was some kind of wild animal trying to get out of a pen."

She paused again, then said, "I don't think it ever crossed Jesse's mind that Bud wouldn't live forever. He couldn't get his mind around his daddy being gone."

Her face darkened, she leaned toward Claire, her gray head shaking with emotion. "That's when he started drinking." She choked out the words as if she were speaking of another death. Tears clouded her sparkling eyes. She took her glasses off and hastily dashed them away.

Claire waited. Mrs. Lola Faye drew a shuddery breath before she spoke again. "He stopped writing, stopped calling. I'd try to get a hold of him, and if he did answer the phone he was always so..." She bit her lower lip and looked intently at Jesse's picture, still in Claire's hand. "It was like he was trying to wash everything away with liquor. His memories, his daddy, how bad he hurt. But he just about got swept away, too."

Mrs. Lola Faye began wringing her hands, causing the dark blue veins to stand out from her pale, thin skin. Claire covered the gnarled hands in her own smooth ones. Their tortured movement stopped and Mrs. Lola Faye composed herself. She smiled up at Claire. "Then one day, I heard the doorbell ring. It was Jesse." For the first time, Mrs. Lola Faye managed a small laugh. "He was poor as a snake but I didn't care what he looked like so long as he was home. He stayed with me for a long time. Went to those A. A. meetings they have in the basement of the Methodist Church. With God's help, he got himself well."

Claire smiled gently, "Jesse must be a very strong

person." Mrs. Lola Faye nodded. "He sure had gone through it up there in Montana. Don't talk about it much at all, kind of like a soldier back from war, you know. But I don't pry. I knew he was back to his old self when he started getting that ramblin' urge. One day he said, 'Momma, I think it's time I headed out. I promise I won't go so far this time.' He found that job up in the northern part of the state and he's doing real good now." She smiled and her face creased into a hundred happy folds.

"I'm so glad, Mrs. Lola Faye." Compassion for this dear lady welled up in Claire's heart and tears began to slip down her cheeks and fall onto the red-and-white checked plastic table cloth.

Mrs. Lola Faye looked alarmed. "Well, Sugar, I didn't mean to upset you."

"Oh, no, Mrs. Lola Faye. I'm just really glad you felt like you could tell me your story. I'm so happy things worked out for Jesse and for you."

Mrs. Lola Faye leaned across the table and patted Claire on the shoulder affectionately. She stood up a little stiffly and made her way to the oven, house-shoes scuffling across the floor as she went. "I think our chicken potpie is just about ready. You hungry?"

They ate in friendly silence. Claire felt humbled to be trusted with hearing Mrs. Lola Faye's story of the storm that had bent, but not broken, her. She decided right then and there to do anything she could to help this woman who had suffered much, but loved more.

****

When Claire shuffled slowly and carefully into the kitchen the next morning, Gran turned around from the stove and eyed her. "Looks like you overdid it at Mrs. Lola Faye's. You're all stove up. Well, cripple on over to the table and eat you some breakfast." As usual, she and Paw had beaten the sun in rising and had eaten long before Claire awoke. Gran fixed a plate of leftover bacon and hash browns and gave it to Claire with a heaping side of unsolicited advice about the foolishness of overexertion.

"Gran," Claire sighed, "It's not like I did it on purpose."

Gran pursed her lips, causing the wrinkles around them to multiply tenfold and took a sip of coffee, "Well, you oughta knowed you wasn't used to hard work."

46

Claire considered arguing that nursing school was very hard work, but thinking about school reminded her of all the worries she'd tried to scrub away at Mrs. Lola Faye's. She nodded mutely and let Gran have her victory.

Paw came in, trailing a cloud of Old Spice aftershave. His steel gray hair was wet and combed over to one side. He had on his best pair of Wranglers and a neatly ironed, striped shirt with silver snaps. Claire recognized his stockyard outfit immediately.

"Where's the sale today?" she asked.

"Glenwood," he replied, gathering a handful of toothpicks and peppermints, stuffing them in his pocket. "You goin'?"

"Sure. Just let me get ready." Claire dressed as quickly as she could in a pair of faded jeans, a pale pink t-shirt, and her grubby tennis shoes. She followed Paw onto the front porch and Gran bustled after them. Claire eased down the steps and discovered she had many more muscles in her legs than she'd previously thought. They were all protesting being called into action again so suddenly. Gran stood watching, her head cocked to the left as it often was when she was thinking.

"Claire," she stopped and looked intently into her granddaughter's face. "Mrs. Lola Faye ain't got any grandchildren and that's a shame. 'Cause if she had one like you, she'd be a lucky woman."

Claire smiled at her grandmother and said, "Well, Mrs. Lola Faye thinks I take after you."

Gran laughed merrily. "Pshaw!" she said, as she disappeared back into the house.

Claire followed Paw to where his gray pickup sat in the driveway. He'd already hooked up to his old trailer, which might have also been gray in years past, but now was a dirty brown color from being endlessly spattered with dirt and manure. Paw didn't care. He wasn't out to impress anyone with his rig which he'd often say when another bidder at the auctions rolled up in a shiny new pickup and matching trailer.

They settled in for the hour-and-a-half long trip to Glenwood. Claire remembered thinking, as a little girl, that it was the longest ride she'd ever taken. Claire couldn't resist the urge to press her nose to the glass and look at the little smudge it left. As a little girl, she used to amuse herself by making nose prints all over Paw's window. She never said a word. She would press her nose to the window as they rolled along past grazing cattle and shining hay fields. It was how she passed the time until Jill's Burger Bar came into view. Paw would grind the truck to a lower gear and start slowing down. Without a word, he'd pull into the little dairy bar, order two vanilla ice cream cones, and climb back in the truck. Claire would race him to see who could finish first, she always won. It occurred to her now that Paw probably let her win, or at least didn't try to beat her, and saved himself an ice cream headache in the process.

She smiled at the memory and carefully wiped the smudge off the window. The clatter of the empty trailer and a Willie Nelson tape kept them company as they rode along. Paw never was much of a talker, although whether by choice or because he couldn't get a word in edgewise with Gran was a matter of community debate.

"Talked to your daddy the other day," he finally said.

"Yeah, I know. I had supper with him that night." Claire's stomach knotted as she remembered her evening with her father, and that her résumé was probably being reviewed this very moment somewhere at Dallas Presbyterian Hospital. She'd wanted to talk to her father about her apprehension, how desperate she'd been for him to understand her misgivings.

They passed by Jill's Burger Bar, and Claire felt a pang of disappointment on seeing it was closed. She realized she'd been looking forward to sharing an ice-cream cone with Paw. *Don't be silly, Claire. Paw probably doesn't even remember that.*

"They open later now."

Claire looked her grandfather, who was fiddling with the toothpick in his mouth and looking straight down the road. "What, Paw?"

"Jill's. They don't open so early now. We'll have to get our ice cream on the way home."

If it wouldn't have scared him to death and embarrassed him besides, Claire would've just squeezed Paw to pieces. He did remember and the knot in her stomach relaxed.

She hesitated before she said anything, chose her words

carefully, and tried them several times in her mind before she attempted putting a voice behind them.

"Why d'ya think Dad's so dead set on me having a job that makes lots of money? That's what 'making it' means, when he says it, anyway. I'm not sure about some stuff, and I don't think he'd listen if I talked to him about it. He's determined I'm going to...to...I really don't understand him at all!" She finished hurriedly, her color and her voice rising with exasperation.

Paw drove on, switching the splintered toothpick for a peppermint. As the silence lengthened, Claire began to regret her outburst. When he finally spoke, she wondered if maybe he wasn't going to acknowledge what she'd said at all.

"Them boys at school used to call your daddy 'Floods.'"

She glanced at him, confused by this seemingly random remark.

"Why'd they do that?" she ventured.

Paw rolled the mint over and over in his jaw, making a lump in his cheek. "The boys would follow him around sayin', 'Must be a flood on the Burke farm. That why your pants is so short?'"

Paw swallowed hard. "He had to wear the same pants for a long time after they'd done got too short. Millie made him shirts outta flour sacks lots of times. Never has been easy makin' a livin' on the farm, but it was real hard back when Frank Jr. was a boy. Other folks had jobs in Pickens and whatnot to go with their farmin', but I didn't. Frank Jr. went without more than most kids but we done the best we knew how to do."

Willie Nelson's plaintive voice sounded the last strains of 'You Were Always on My Mind,' and the tape whirred into silence. Paw turned it over in the player and said nothing else.

Now it was Claire's turn to stare down the road in silence. Her chest constricted at the thought of her father, just a little boy, being laughed at and taunted for something he couldn't help. He'd harnessed every ounce of ability and determination he possessed to make a life that included all the things he'd lacked as a child. She was sad for his suffering and also for his grandiose attempts to make up for it.

She snuck a quick look at Paw. His big, rough hands rested on top of the steering wheel and he seemed absorbed in his driving. The peppermint turned slowly around and around in his mouth, while Claire's thoughts did the same in her mind.

****

The Grant County Livestock Auction was held, just as it had been when Claire was a child, in a huge two-story wooden building. The graying white paint was peeling more than Claire remembered, but other than that, it was just the same.

Paw pulled into his favorite parking spot under a sweet gum tree at the far right side of the gravel parking lot. They picked their way through potholes made by the trailer traffic and cow piles from the occupants of those trailers.

Claire pushed open the front door and suddenly, she was seven years old again. The aroma of frying beef wafted from the little concession stand. In her mind's eye, she could see Paw bending over to place a warm napkin-wrapped cheeseburger in her small hands.

Overriding the concession stand aroma was the pungent, heavy scent of hundreds of cattle. Their bawling pierced the air as they were herded into holding pens in the back of the building.

Paw was making his way through the crowd of buyers, most of whom acknowledged him with a nod or a slightly lifted hand. Paw returned their mild greetings in kind and pressed on through the echoing concrete tunnel that led under the bidders' seats and up to a narrow, battered wooden door at the back of the building. Behind the door was an even narrower staircase. The steps were uneven and dimly lit, with wide gaps between them. Claire grabbed Paw's elbow as they climbed.

They reached the top of the stairs and stepped onto a platform that looked down into the holding pens. A few small, grimy windows allowed just a touch of outside light to filter in, as she blinked to adjust her eyes to the semi-darkness.

Claire stepped very carefully onto the maze of wooden walkways that twisted and turned through the dusty air. She clutched the rough hewn handrails and looked down, half afraid, half mesmerized by what she saw.

A sea of brown, red, black, tan, white, and yellow hide was flowing below them like a living river. An occasional cowboy hat whipped by, like debris caught in the fast moving current, concealing its hollering wearer from her bird's eye view.

Clouds of dark brown dirt rose and filled the air with a dry, acrid smell as the cowboys herded, yelled, and cursed cattle of every size and description into their appropriate pens with heifers and steers here, bulls here, mama cows with calves over there.

They eased along the catwalks, Paw quietly inspecting the sea of animals that swirled below him and Claire clinging to his shirttail, trying to keep her eyes on where she placed her feet. Through the large gaps between the walkway planks, the motion of the animals sweeping along below them made Claire dizzy.

After Paw decided which animals he planned to bid on, they made their way back down the steep stairwell and up the concrete bleachers that formed a coliseum style semi-circle around the selling pen.

Claire looked around at the slowly gathering crowd. Most were men about Paw's age, with graying hair edging out from under their hats. Many had spit-cups in their hands and Skoal rings on the back pockets of their Wranglers. Those who didn't wear cowboy hats had on caps that advertised John Deere tractors, McCallister's Feed, J & T Saddles, or similar farming slogans.

Paw's sharp eyes also surveyed the cavernous room, narrowing slightly when they rested upon a man he thought might engage him in a bidding war. He pulled a small rectangular piece of paper from his shirt pocket and tapped it on his palm. It was his bidding card, his weapon of choice for today's contest. He was ready.

A short, bowlegged man with an oversized hat stepped out into the enclosed booth above the sale ring that served as the auctioneer's stand. He took a swig of Coke, swished it around in his mouth and spit on the dirt. Settling himself onto the backless stool that stood behind a low metal table, he picked up a microphone and tapped it with a stubby finger.

"Testing, testing," His voice held a whine like a motor laboring to shift into a higher gear. "Y'all ready?"

The low humming of voices grew quieter and the bawling of the cattle increased to a fevered pitch. Thundering hooves and yelling cowhands could be heard in the back of the barn as the first animal up for bidding came barreling down the narrow corridors Claire had peered into a few moments ago.

A pair of large metal doors swung open and a burly Black Angus bull lumbered into the sale ring below the auctioneer's perch. He slung his head wildly from side to side, spinning around in a vain attempt to charge the cowboy who had ushered him into the arena. The cowboy was too quick and, with a catlike leap, he perched himself on the tall iron fence that separated the people from the livestock.

Paw leaned forward and watched the bull wheeling around the ring, blowing its displeasure in great wet bursts from its nostrils. "That's a fool," he said. "Don't want none of that blood in your herd."

Claire had been staring mesmerized at the huge bull, watching its muscles ripple under the taut black hide as it whirled around and around.

"Are you getting rid of Charles?" She hoped Paw hadn't come to the sale to find a replacement for his aging, grumpy Simmental bull. She'd always liked sullen, old Charles.

"Nah. He's getting' on up there in years, but his last bunch of calves was still good-sized. He ain't too old yet. I'm buying for that Hightower feller that lives over on the old Nugent place. He's got him a few cows and wants to start raising some calves." Paw was the Grant County expert on all things bovine. Other farmers often sought his expertise in selecting, doctoring, and selling their cattle.

Claire leaned her sore back onto the bench behind her and watched as two men on opposite sides of the sale barn silently and stealthily tried to outbid each other. A stocky man on the bottom row bid on the Angus first by barely raising an index finger. His bid was acknowledged by the auctioneer, whose motor had shifted into its highest gear and was racing along with a plaintive, insistent tone.

The stocky man was challenged by a bald, heavyset fellow on the top row to Claire's left, who bid by nodding his head very slightly at the auctioneer. The auctioneer's hawk eyes continually swept the crowd, watching for the slightest sign of motion that could indicate a bid being made.

Claire wondered if anyone ever went to scratch his nose and ended up buying a cow. The next thing she knew, the snorting bull was poked and prodded out of the arena and another one was tumbling in from behind the metal doors.

Paw perked up at the sight of the gray Brahman. Its pearly black horns curved neatly upward above its long floppy ears. The big hump on its back swayed from side to side as the bull calmly circled the ring.

"Hightower said he might like a Bremmer bull." Paw let the bidding run for a few seconds before he made a barely noticeable, upward motion with the white card he held propped on his knee. Claire made out "Burke, nine fifty," in the buzzing of the auctioneer's words. The Brahman continued to saunter lazily around the ring, until the auctioneer suddenly banged his gavel like a judge and pronounced the bull "Sold to Burke for nine seventy-five."

Paw leaned back, pocketing his bidding card like a gunslinger holstering his pistol. He remained in this attitude of quiet triumph until the cow and calf pairs began selling, then drew his bidding card and resumed his tensed and ready position on the edge of the bleacher.

By the end of the day, Claire had gained a new appreciation for cushioned seating while Paw had successfully bid on not just the Brahman bull for Mr. Hightower, but also an orphaned calf that had been run through the ring at the end of the auction. Its mother, Paw told her, had probably died during birth and the farmer who owned her didn't have time to fool with raising a bottle calf.

After Paw paid for his animals in the small, cigarette-smoke-clouded business office, Claire followed him into the brilliant midday sun. He pulled the trailer around back to the loading chute, where two teenaged boys in dirty jeans and torn t-shirts loaded the bull and the calf into the trailer.

The bull strolled to the front of the trailer, languidly rested his chin on the bars and looked as if he hadn't a care in the world. The calf was much more nervous. She darted anxiously from one side of the trailer to the other, sticking her head out through the bars and bawling pitifully.

Paw closed the trailer door with a clang and they set off for the old Nugent place to present the Hightowers with their new bull. Claire spent much of the ride home facing backward, trying to see how the calf was handling the ride. The little heifer was standing stiff-legged with her delicate pink hooves firmly planted on the slatted wood floor to keep from being flung around when the trailer turned, sped up, or slowed down. Claire looked at the calf's anxious brown eyes, wide with confusion and fear, and decided this little heifer would be hers. She would give it a bottle and take care of it for as long as she was at her grandparents'.

By the time they got to Dogwood, Paw and Claire had both finished their ice cream cones and Claire was wishing she'd bought something to drink at Jill's Burger Bar.

The road began to slope gently downward as they rolled past Paw's house and on toward the Nugent place. After a couple of miles, Paw slowed the truck and turned onto a gravel road that wound through a stand of trees. The land leveled off and Claire could see lush grass and tangles of flowering weeds through the gaps in the pines.

The trees opened up suddenly and they were driving along the edge of an expansive field. A small, brick house, so far away it looked like a doll's house, stood to one side of the field. They headed toward it, following a long driveway that passed a red barn, a tractor shed, and several staring cows and calves. As they drew closer, Claire could see that the ground beyond the house dropped suddenly away. She guessed this must be the river.

"Paw, isn't this where Mrs. Lola Faye lived?" she asked as they stopped in front of the house.

"Yeah. She sold it when Bud died. Took a while to find a buyer, but then these people showed up from somewhere. Wyoming or some place like that. I thought it was a man and wife for a long time, but turns out it's a woman and her brother. She's got a boy, too, but I don't reckon she's married. They keep to themselves, mostly."

With that, Paw climbed out of the truck, strode up the steps, and knocked on the front door. Claire noticed a wheelchair ramp running parallel with the porch steps.

After a few minutes, the door opened just a crack. It was enough for Claire to see a woman in a wheelchair peering through the screen door. Paw asked her something and she pointed toward the tractor barn. Paw nodded and started in the direction the woman had pointed. She shut the door quickly and was gone.

Paw trekked through the tall grass toward the barn to ask William Hightower where to unload the bull. He was gone for quite a while, and when he finally reappeared, there was a grim and determined look on his face.

"They got a cow trying to deliver a breech calf," he said through the open truck window. "Gonna have to pull it, looks like. Hightower needs some help. May take a while." Paw got a length of rope from the back of the truck and headed back toward the barn at a brisk pace.

Claire looked at the house, the ramp, and the tightly shut screen door. She was getting terribly thirsty. The lady in the wheelchair didn't seem overly friendly but Claire's parched throat demanded she ask for a drink.

She knocked softly, and after what seemed like a very long time, the wooden door behind the screen eased open. Claire found herself facing a very stiff, straight-backed woman. Everything about her was straight, from her thin nose to her shoulder-length, light brown hair. Even her unsmiling lips and the way she sat in her wheel chair, as if she were a soldier who'd just been called to attention, were straight.

"Can I help you?" Her clipped words lacked the softening southern drawl so often heard in Dogwood. Claire peered through the screen door and said, "Hi. I'm Claire, Mr. Burke's granddaughter. I've been waiting in the truck and he just came to say he was going to help pull a calf." The woman looked at her with a watchful, wary gaze. Claire finished hastily, "I was wondering if I could have a glass of water."

She regarded Claire thoughtfully for a moment. "I can bring you something. Or would you like to come in?" Claire said she'd just stay on the porch, thinking the woman didn't seem in the mood for company just then. Or ever. Not to mention the fact she had just spent the better part of the day at a sale barn where aromas seemed to be attracted to fabric.

The woman returned, wheeled out onto the porch, and handed Claire a glass of ice water. She watched her drink it with a guarded, cautious expression. Claire finished the water and handed the glass back with a quick thank you. She was turning to leave when the woman said suddenly, "I'm Deloris Hightower. Why don't you have a seat?"

Deloris gestured towards a lawn chair on the porch. As she sat down, Claire looked at Deloris closely, immediately noticing her eyes. They were a golden-green color, like a cat's eyes. The more Claire thought about it, the more Deloris Hightower reminded her of a wild, stray cat she'd tried to befriend at her grandparents' house when she was a girl. It would come just close enough for Claire to brush its fur with her fingertips, but never close enough to really touch.

They sat in awkward silence for a moment, Claire cast around in her mind for an ice-breaker. Her eyes swept across the fields around them. They were sprinkled with Black-eyed Susans, each a bright burst of sunshine against the vibrant green Bermuda grass.

"This is a really pretty place."

"Thank you," she answered with obvious pride. "We like it here. It's especially nice in the spring when the wildflowers are blooming."

Claire ventured another comment. "My grandfather said you moved here from Wyoming or somewhere." She only mentioned it because relocating to a completely different setting was on her mind of late, and she wondered how Deloris had ended up here.

Her mouth went rigidly straight in an instant. Claire realized she'd touched a nerve, although she couldn't imagine why.

Claire opened her mouth to apologize, but before she could say anything, a little boy's voice broke the silence. "It's a bull calf! And it's alive!"

Claire looked to see a little boy running towards them at full tilt. His black rubber boots slapped against bare, sun-browned legs as he galloped along. A wide, joyous smile was plastered across his face and his bright green eyes sparkled with excitement. He was almost to the porch when he finally noticed Claire and came to a sudden halt. She recognized him as Joshua, the boy she'd seen racing around the tree at church with Sage Finley's little girl.

"Hey. Who're you?" he asked breathlessly.

"Joshua!" Deloris said in a warning tone. "Don't forget your manners."

Joshua answered with a penitent, "Yes, Ma'am," then addressed Claire again. "Hello. I'm Joshua Hightower. Very nice to meet you, Miss."

The little boy's freshly adopted, dapper manners were charming. They contrasted so thoroughly with his wind-tossed blonde hair and dirty knees, Claire wanted to laugh. She almost expected him to bow deeply from the waist, and if he had been wearing a cap he'd have surely doffed it with a sweeping gesture.

Deloris, too, was amused by her little boy's gentlemanly turn and, for the first time, Claire saw a real smile on her face. She had not realized until that moment Deloris Hightower was a very pretty woman and not nearly as old as she'd first thought. Claire suspected the fine wrinkles that rested on her high cheekbones were more from care and worry than age. She noticed a wide jagged scar, faded by time to a pallid white, running across Deloris's neck. Claire tried not to stare and turned her eyes quickly back to Joshua.

"Hello, Joshua. I'm Claire. It's nice to meet you, too. Did you help deliver the calf?"

"Yeah," Joshua replied, forgetting his lofty manners in an instant. He plopped down on the porch next to his mother's chair. Claire watched as Deloris rumpled the boy's hair and smiled to herself.

"Uncle William thought it'd be dead when they got it out, but it's doin' good. Mr. Burke knows lots about cows. He knew how to get it out and that momma cow's gonna live, too, looks like." He nodded triumphantly, proud to be the bearer of good news. "Now I've gotta go help them unload that ol' bull and give him his shots."

Joshua dashed away and joined Paw and William Hightower as they got in the truck and started pulling the trailer back toward the barn.

Claire looked back at Deloris and was happy to see Joshua's brightening effect on his mother remained. Affection warmed her voice as she said, "I've never seen a little boy who loves animals more than Joshua. He's just like..."

She stopped abruptly and clamped her lips together, as if she were physically restraining something from slipping out of her mouth. "Just like his uncle," she finished.

Hurriedly changing the subject, she asked, "Do you live with your grandparents? I don't know many people in

Dogwood, but I don't remember seeing you with Mr. Burke before."

Claire explained she wouldn't be staying long and would probably soon be leaving the state for parts unknown. She told Deloris about seeing Joshua at church the previous Sunday.

Deloris seemed keenly interested in this small fact, although Claire couldn't imagine why.

"Do you know many people at the church?"

"No, not really. I know Mrs. Lola Faye Nugent pretty well."

Deloris raised her eyebrows and leaned forward in her chair, but said nothing. Claire went on. "And Brother Jake, of course."

"I really like Brother Jake. He's a true man of God," Deloris said, with uncharacteristic gentleness.

Claire was surprised that such a reclusive woman as Deloris Hightower had dealings with Jake Weston. She began to think about Sage's comment that her neighbor was homebound. True, Deloris was in a wheelchair but Claire knew plenty of people in wheelchairs who weren't confined to their homes. There seemed to be nothing physical keeping Deloris at home. Claire was growing more and more puzzled by this enigmatic person, but her musings were soon interrupted by the sound of a vehicle approaching.

Claire could see a familiar brown pickup stirring up a cloud of dust as it rumbled down the long driveway. *Speak of the devil,* Claire unconsciously began smoothing her wayward hair, *I guess I'll find out how she knows Brother Jake after all.*

Jake got out of his truck with his usual grin. It widened ever so slightly when he saw Claire on the porch and his hazel eyes registered pleasant surprise.

"Well, hello, Claire. Deloris, how're you doing today?"

Jake bounded up onto the porch, completely forgoing the steps. "Here you go," he said, handing a cassette tape to Deloris. "Last Sunday's sermon, just like always."

Deloris thanked him and asked how Joshua was behaving at church. After reassuring her Joshua was minding his manners impeccably, Jake turned to Claire.

"What brings you to the banks of the Hearn River today?"

Claire told him about her trip to the stockyard with Paw and the subsequent calf-pulling drama that had unfolded in the barn. "Now they've gone to get the new bull vaccinated and settled in," she finished, realizing she was probably intruding on a pastoral visit and should make herself scarce.

She thanked Deloris for letting her pass the time on her porch and excused herself with the intention of going to the trailer, now parked in front of the barn, to see how her orphaned calf was doing.

Claire walked with a stiff, slightly bow-legged gait down the sidewalk. When she turned to wave one final good-bye, she noticed Jake was fighting mightily to contain a laugh.

"OK, Preacher, what's so funny?"

"You're walking like a cowboy who's just come in from a weeklong cattle drive. Have you been on a trail ride or something?"

Claire could see the sparkle in Jake's eyes. While she wouldn't take kidding from just anyone, for some reason it didn't bother her for Jake to tease her but she wasn't going to let him know that. She replied huffily, "For your information, I overdid it a bit when I was cleaning for Mrs. Lola Faye yesterday."

Claire continued, hands on her hips. "I most certainly have not been on a trail ride. There's no way you'll ever catch me on a horse. I don't ride things that can think. I'll stick to four-wheelers. They're not going to decide to wade out in the middle of the pond and stay there for three hours while you're yelling your head off for someone to come help you. Plus, they don't have saddles that come undone and send you sliding down a hill on your backside! *And* they won't sneeze in your hair while you're trying to pet them and scare you to death. Have you ever had a horse sneeze on you? It's really loud. *And* wet! *And* not very sanitary, I imagine." Claire was just getting warmed up recalling the traumas she'd suffered from a stubborn pony her grandparents had owned when she was cut short by a gale of laughter.

Jake and Deloris finally managed to contain their mirth. "I used to love riding horses before my accident," Deloris said, looking down at her wheelchair with an expression steeped in regret.

No one spoke. Deloris looked off into the distance, as if watching something only her eyes could see. Jake waited patiently for her to speak. Claire surmised he knew much more about Deloris Hightower's past than anyone else in Dogwood.

Deloris came out of her reverie with a start. She shook her head, clearing away whatever cloud had darkened her mind.

"I need to get back to my housework." She eased her chair backward, paused before entering the house and briefly looked from Claire to Jake and back again. "You two can stay out here and enjoy each other's company, if you like." Then she was gone.

Claire looked at the screen door, still vibrating from Deloris' exit. "What was that all about?"

Jake sighed, ran his fingers through his hair, and rubbed his chin, which Claire had gathered meant he was deep in thought. "I've been visiting Deloris Hightower since I came to Dogwood, and I can tell you this much—she's a hard lady to know. I'm sure you gathered that. Lots of things in her past that..."

Claire saw a look of sorrow darken his usually sunny face. A pastor has many burdens to bear, and most of them are other people's, she realized.

Jake turned and looked at Claire, "I can't really say much. Confidential pastor stuff, you know."

"Like attorney-client privilege?" she asked, smiling.

"Something like that. God forgives us much more easily than we forgive ourselves, sometimes."

Jake sat brooding for a few moments, then asked Claire if she would like a ride home. "After all," he said, "you never know how long Mr. Burke will be out there in the barn and I'm going by your place anyway."

"Well, Deloris probably doesn't want me to come in and visit, and I don't particularly want to spend the afternoon on this porch, so..." Claire tried not to sound too eager as she agreed to let Jake drop her off at her grandparents' house.

She controlled a strong urge to skip to the truck, her stiff legs greatly helped with that resolve. Jake looked dubiously at Claire as she tried to maneuver into his jacked-up truck. "Here," he said, laughing, "let me help you." He took her hand in his and helped Claire into the seat. "We'll drive out to the barn and tell Mr. Burke I'm taking you home."

As he shut the door and started around to the driver's side, Claire allowed herself the tiniest, quietest fit of hand-clapping imaginable. By the time, Jake slid into place behind the steering wheel, she was perfectly composed again. No one was the wiser about her excited little outburst.

****

Deloris watched them make their way to the truck from her bedroom window. As they pulled away, she let the curtain fall back into place. In her hands, she held a faded picture of a smiling, young man sitting astride a Palomino and grinning widely. She pressed the picture to her heart, then placed it back in its hiding place in a dresser drawer. She smiled and listened to the noise of Joshua's whooping and hollering as he rode his stick-horse around and around the house.

Chapter Eight

Gran was sitting on the front porch, shucking corn. Her fingers trailed strings of sticky, corn silk that stuck to her nose as she readjusted her glasses and tried to appear uninterested in the occupants of the brown truck that had just pulled into the front yard.

After Jake and Claire had talked for a few moments, she slid out of the truck and started up the sidewalk. Jake waved to Gran, who made a great show of being busy, barely pausing in her vigorous shucking to raise an ear of corn in response. As Jake drove away, Claire eased up the porch steps, smiling to herself, and started into the house. Gran hummed something that sounded suspiciously like "Love Is a Many Splendored Thing." Claire paused as she passed the perfectly still porch swing and looked at her grandmother. "Not a word, Gran!"

Gran stared at her with wide eyes and lifted her hands innocently. "Not a word about what?" she asked, and began trying in earnest to de-silk her nose.

When Paw finally returned from the Hightower farm, he pulled off his sweaty, dirty cap, rubbed his head wearily, and sank into his La-Z-Boy in front of the television.

"Paw, where did you put the calf?" Claire asked.

"Under the shed on the north side of the barn," Paw replied, thickly. The emergency delivery he'd performed for the Hightower's cow had worn him out. Claire was about to ask if the calf was doing alright, but Paw's head slumped onto his chest before she could say another word. Rumbling snores followed her as she snuck out the backdoor and made her way to the barn.

The sun had already started its downward slide as she walked the worn footpath. The sweet smell of hay greeted her as she peered through the gate bars at the tiny calf, curled next to the bales that kept residence in the shed.

"Hello, Little One," Claire called softly as she slowly

climbed the gate and perched on the top bar. She noticed a bottle, much like a baby's bottle, but over a foot tall and with a stiff, black nipple several inches long. On lifting it, she was surprised to find it was heavy with warm milk. Paw must have planned to feed the calf after he'd rested for a while. *I can do it for him. After all, I did decide I'd take care of the poor little thing.*

The calf raised and lowered its feathery white lashes at Claire as she approached with the bottle. She knelt on the prickly hay and gingerly extended the bottle toward the calf's pearly pink nose. It gave the bottle a disinterested sniff and turned its head. Claire moved the bottle toward the calf's mouth, and the heifer promptly turned her head again. Claire repositioned the bottle and tried to coax the calf into drinking.

"Here you go, Charlotte." The name came to her at that very moment. It suited the calf, she decided, because it was a delicate and gentle sounding name.

Claire stuck the bottle right against the calf's tightly shut mouth. Charlotte, taking umbrage at this liberty on her caregiver's part, let out a loud, plaintive bawl and stood up.

"It's OK," Claire reassured, taking a step toward the calf as it backed into the corner of the barn. "Just take a little milk and you'll feel better." Claire advanced another step, and Charlotte lowered her head and tried to look like an intimidating, raging menace about to charge. Claire was taken aback, but not at all frightened. "Well, alright then, we'll just have to do this the hard way," she said, reaching for the calf.

Charlotte made a break for it and darted to the other side of the barn. When Claire cornered her again, the calf was ready. Claire made a dive, intending to catch Charlotte by the head. The calf anticipated her move and ran in the other direction, leaving Claire grasping a handful of tail. Charlotte broke free and Claire gave chase, the bottle tucked under her arm, milk running down her jeans.

She cornered the calf again, and stood panting and staring at the feisty creature. Its nostrils flared and Claire imagined if a calf could scowl then Charlotte was giving her the dirtiest of looks at that very moment. She looked at the snorting, determined little heifer and wondered how to proceed. With a loud, defiant bawl, Charlotte darted past

Claire's legs and wedged herself between two hay bales with nothing but her bright white hind-end sticking out.

Hot, sweaty, and annoyed, Claire stalked toward the switching white tail. Charlotte was cornered and knew it. She gave a kick, but missed as Claire wrapped her arms around the calf's legs and pulled. Charlotte fell mooing to the floor and Claire hauled her out from between the bales triumphantly. She sat straddling the calf's neck and shoved the bottle into her bawling mouth. Charlotte sputtered indignantly for a few seconds before she began sucking down the milk with abandon.

"There!" Claire said, hay sticking out of her hair and dirt smeared on her face. "If you'd just do what I say and not fight me, things would be a lot easier on both of us." The calf made no apologies. Claire continued to chide and pet the calf in the now quiet shed, listening to the gentle, rhythmic swallowing sounds of Charlotte emptying her bottle.

Just as Charlotte drained the bottle, Claire became aware of someone watching her. Her back was to the gate, but she felt eyes on her. She turned her head slowly, expecting to see Paw or Gran.

She let out a little screech when she saw Jake resting his arms over the gate and watching her with a look she couldn't quite decipher.

Claire's scream startled Charlotte, who leapt up with a power one wouldn't suspect possible from such a fragile looking creature. Her sudden escape sent Claire sprawling.

Lying on her back, Claire looked up at the rafters and wished with all her might she'd just had a hallucination and Jake hadn't been watching her. She put her hand over her eyes and discovered it was covered with something she sincerely hoped was only mud. She wiped it on her jeans as Jake's face appeared above her.

"How much did you see?" Claire asked with a groan.

"Enough to know you're quite a cowgirl. Too bad they don't take women in the steer wrestling part of the rodeo. You've got a future if you could just polish your technique."

Taking her dirty hand, he pulled her up. Their hands stayed joined together for a few moments longer than necessary until Claire pulled hers away awkwardly.

"So, what're you doing here? I mean, at the barn. It's not like I'm trying to tell you where you can or can't be. I'm just surprised to see you down here. I thought I was alone and Charlotte didn't want to take her bottle and I really don't know how to feed a calf," She paused in her flustered rambling and looked at his wide smile. "I guess you've come to visit Gran and Paw. They're at the house, "

He reached over and took a piece of hay from her hair. "No, I'm here to see you."

Claire looked into his face and tried to read his expression. "Why?" she asked.

"I'm going into the woods to shoot some stuff. Thought you might like to come."

She opened her mouth in horror, but quickly shut it again as Jake laughed and pointed to a camera sitting by the gate. "Pictures. That's about all I shoot. Your paw has got some really nice trails through the woods on the back of the place. He showed me around a few years back and said I could ride whenever I wanted."

"Riding?" Claire asked nervously. The last thing she needed was the chance Jake would see her land on her rear again, and she dearly hoped he didn't mean to take her anywhere on horseback.

"Relax. I won't forget your sentiments about horses anytime soon. I have an old clunker four-wheeler I like to knock around on." He looked down at his feet for a split second. "It's big enough for you to ride with me...I mean, if you want to, of course," he said with a hint of bashfulness.

She opened the gate and clanged it shut behind them. Charlotte, who suddenly had a magnetic attraction to the bottle, bawled indignantly as Jake and Claire started toward the house. "I just need to tell Gran where I'm going so she won't think I've fallen in the pond and drowned or something."

Jake kicked up a small cloud of dust with his shoes and cut his eyes at Claire walking beside him. "Actually, she already knows where we're going. I stopped to look for you at the house and she told me where you might be. She saw the four-wheeler in the truck and," he paused and looked at her apologetically, "Mrs. Millie has a way of getting information out of a person, I guess. I told her what I'd come to ask you. I hope you don't mind."

Claire sighed, and Jake looked at her with concern.

"You're not mad, are you?" he asked quickly.

"No," Claire laughed, noting his worry with a hint of pleasure. "I just don't know what I'm going to do with Gran. She knows I'm going to be leaving soon, but she's bound and determined to…well…you know," she finished lamely.

They continued their slow stroll towards the farm house. "Know what?" he asked.

It was Claire's turn to feel bashful as she bit her bottom lip and tried to phrase her reply in the breeziest, most flippant manner possible. "Well, it's silly, really, but I think Gran has got it into her head that we…" she paused and rolled her eyes skyward, seeking some help from the cloudless azure sky. None appeared, so she pressed on again with her determined airiness. "That you and I should…I don't know how to put it."

"Start seeing each other, maybe?" Jake ventured, hesitantly.

Claire stood stock still and watched him. He took a few more steps before turning to face her.

"Yeah, I guess you could put it that way," she said with a forced laughed. "Isn't that crazy?" Her smile was painfully false as she waited for his reply.

He walked back to where she had stopped and said, "Is it?" His face was as serious as she'd ever seen it, and her mind whirled in a dizzying circle.

"I really have enjoyed your company, but you're settled in here and I'm going to be moving away soon. That's really why I came this summer, you know. To say good-bye, kind of. I wouldn't want to start seeing someone, anyone, really, and then leave and…" her voice trailed off.

Jake's pained expression passed as quickly as it came, and he nodded with a tightlipped smile.

"Mrs. Millie is a strong-minded lady. When she takes a notion, she really clings to it." Claire laughed uneasily and they walked on in uncomfortable silence.

She could see Gran watching their approach from behind a wall of wet sheets on the clothesline. Claire's arms were crossed tightly against her chest as she walked with her eyes on the ground, and Jake's stiff body language looked just as uneasy. Gran shook her head, collected her laundry basket and clothespins, and stomped into the house.

When they reached the yard, Jake pulled a pair of homemade ramps from the bed of his truck and began backing his ragged four-wheeler onto the ground. Like the truck it came in, the wheeler had seen better days. Its fenders had long since been broken off, and Jake had replaced them with makeshift brown ones that didn't match the rest of the faded red paint. The seat was torn in several places, exposing the foam padding inside. A rickety, wooden box was bolted onto the front rack to hold Jake's camera. The only thing new about the whole rig was a small cushy seat mounted carefully on the back.

"I'm ready if you are." He gestured toward the small seat. "I made this so the ride wouldn't be so rough." A faint blush colored his ears as Claire climbed on. She scooted as far back as she could and held on to the bars behind her. The engine sputtered to life with a protesting growl and they were off.

"Sorry about the noise," Jake hollered over his shoulder as they swept along the lane that led to the bottom field. "The muffler's shot."

"It's fine. Really!" Claire yelled.

"Are you comfortable?" Jake bellowed.

There were more levels to that question than he realized. Claire shouted back. "Yeah. I'm good."

They sped down the lane and through the fields, the warm wind pressing against their faces and sweeping away the dust clouding in their wake. Claire began to relax as they went on. She introduced Jake to some of the cows they passed, including the black cow with a white stripe around its middle she'd named Oreo. Jake was impressed with the massive bulk of Charles, but the bull didn't appreciate their puttering around his hay bale. Charles made a lumbering charge toward them and sent them on their way.

The lane began to slope downward and the cow pastures dropped away behind them. Jake slowed their pace. They drove towards a shallow slough, pausing to watch silvery minnows dart for cover among the willow trunks. A turtle watched them approach, then glided soundlessly into the water, leaving only the faintest ripple behind. A blue crane perched on a fallen tree in the shadows by the bank. He shifted from one spindly leg to the other before lifting into the air with a few slow, deliberate flaps.

They eased the four-wheeler into the slough. Steam rose from the engine and the water came up higher than Claire had expected.

"Better put your feet up." Jake shifted into low gear and churned through the slough, leaving a trail of roiling, muddy water behind them.

As they crested the top of the slough's bank, the four-wheeler's right front tire hit a stump. It was slung forcefully onto two wheels, and for a second Claire thought they would turn over.

She instinctively reached for Jake, grabbed him tightly around the waist, and closed her eyes. The ATV bounced back down onto all four tires with a jarring thud.

Claire realized what she was doing the moment the danger was passed, but held onto him for another minute or two anyway.

"That was a close one," he said.

"Crazy men drivers," Claire replied. With her eyes still closed, she didn't notice the twinkle in his eyes.

They slipped through the tree line at the back of the field to a part of the property rarely visited by anyone. A grassy trail wound and curved along, taking them deeper and deeper into the woods. Sunlight filtered lazily through the dense trees and cast an emerald glow on their path. Weaving slowly between the trees, Jake carefully navigated the four-wheeler to a small clearing.

Claire saw they were at the top of a little hill, looking down into a leafy valley. A stream bubbled along below them, singing as it made its way to bigger waters somewhere else.

Jake turned off the engine and pointed up. Above them, twining and twisting through the trees, was a thick canopy of Carolina Jessamine. The bright yellow blossoms made a flowery tent that glowed like the midday sun. The hot air was saturated with their intoxicatingly sweet fragrance.

She looked up in awe, breathing in the beautiful aroma and listening to the singing stream as Jake watched her with a delighted expression.

"How did you know about this place? We must be miles from the back field."

"I found it last summer when I was out wandering around. I like to come here sometimes and sit by myself. If you want to be still and be with God, you can't beat this place."

He climbed off the four-wheeler, and Claire followed. They picked their way down the hill to the sloping banks of the stream. Jake stretched out on a carpet of velvety moss, pillowed his head in his hands and looked up at the saffron trumpet-shaped Jessamine above them. Claire settled in beside him, and gazed into the gently flowing water. Tiny lavender wildflowers, no bigger than raindrops, were sprinkled along the water's edge. Claire picked a miniature bouquet as Jake continued to lay still and quiet, looking up at the golden tangle of blooms.

"I bet we're the only people who've ever seen this. Paw doesn't come this far out when he goes hunting," Claire said.

She rearranged the delicate wildflowers held between her thumb and forefinger and tossed them into the water. They dispersed and drifted away as she let the water ripple between her fingers. She leaned back and looked into the flowers draped above them. "It seems like a waste, doesn't it? For all this to be hidden away and only us getting to see it. If you hadn't found it, it would've bloomed and died and no one would've ever known it was here."

Jake looked steadily at her and said, "If eyes were made for seeing, then beauty is its own excuse for being."

She turned onto her elbow and faced him with a puzzled expression. "What?"

"Ralph Waldo Emerson," he replied, rolling onto his side and looking back at her.

"Ohhh," she said, softly. "I thought maybe that was something you'd just made up."

He looked into her wide green eyes. "I wish."

The woods were silent except for the rustling of leaves overhead and the babbling of the stream at their feet. Claire sat up and hugged her knees to her chest. "I don't think I've ever read that poem."

Jake idly picked a few blades of grass. He stuck one between his teeth and replied, "I like it because every time I read it, I'm reminded there's beauty and purpose in everything God created, just the way it is and just where it is. Even if it's only a flower in the woods that only two people ever get to see. It makes a difference to those two, if they'll let it."

He stopped and looked intently at her. Her eyes were on the stream, and a quiet brooding air hung over her like a cloud. She blinked away a tear, then turned to him and smiled. Getting to her feet, she said, "Thank you for bringing me here. It's lovely."

Jake looked worriedly at Claire, but she brushed off his concern. "I'm fine. Just a little moody, I guess. Maybe I have a poetic streak in me. Aren't artistic types supposed to be kind of difficult and gloomy?"

"I don't know," said Jake, not quite able to mimic Claire's lightened tone. Concern still lingered in his voice as he added, "Only if they have something to be gloomy about, I think."

Claire ignored the question hidden in his words and Jake took the hint. He retrieved his camera from its case, snapped a few pictures of the lush scenery and started the four-wheeler. Claire climbed onto her seat and they headed back towards the farmhouse, leaving their haven to darken with the deepening shadows.

Chapter Nine

Claire sat outside in the porch swing long after Jake went home. She swung slowly in the purple twilight, staring into the gathering night, twirling a curl slowly around her forefinger.

The screen door creaked, bringing Claire out of her reverie. Gran came outside and sat down next to Claire. She patted her on the knee, but said nothing. Gran even helped keep the swing going in its gentle arc as she tried to make out Claire's expression in the darkness.

"Claire..."

She didn't want to hear any lectures or advice or schemes for her happiness. All she wanted was to be alone. Or maybe that was the last thing she wanted.

Claire rested her head on the old woman's shoulders and waited to hear what she would say.

"Claire," Gran began again, "you had two phone calls while you were out."

Claire lifted her head and looked at Gran. The quiet, steady voice made her feel as if Gran were about to break some bad news to her.

"Mrs. Lola Faye wanted to know if you could take her to her post-operative check up tomorrow in Little Rock."

"Sure," said Claire, slowly, wondering if this was what had caused the change in Gran's demeanor. "Who else called?"

Gran sat swinging for a second before she answered. "A man named Jasper Johnson called to set up an interview with you at Dallas Presbyterian Hospital. You're supposed to call him back tomorrow afternoon and let him know when you can come."

Claire heard her own voice murmur "OK." She was certain she should be happy about this. A request for an interview meant he'd been impressed with her résumé. Rita Sparks' glowing recommendation on her behalf had probably helped too. Now she wondered if she'd even call Jasper Johnson back.

A mockingbird flitted by. Its gray and black blurred with the shadows so only the white in its feathers was visible. The bird found its nest somewhere in the tall, oak tree and sang a goodnight serenade, a melancholy medley of songs that struck Claire as being very lonesome.

"I've always thought mockingbirds was kinda sad," Gran said, starting for the door.

Claire looked at her as she stood silhouetted in the dim lamplight that came through the open front door. "Why?"

"Because they're always singing somebody else's song." Gran went into the house and shut the door, leaving Claire alone in the starless night.

****

Claire arrived at Mrs. Lola Faye's bright and early the next morning. She came to see if she could help her elderly friend get ready for their trip, but Mrs. Lola Faye opened the door while Claire's hand was still poised over the doorbell. She was wearing a dress and costume jewelry as she always did when going out, and carried a Mason jar full of ice water along with her purse. "In case I get thirsty," she explained.

Mrs. Lola Faye squared her shoulders and set her lips in a determined line, "Let's get this over with."

At the edge of the porch, Mrs. Lola Faye stopped to pick up a small, potted marigold. She carried it with her and placed it in the backseat of Claire's car so carefully Claire wondered if she might buckle it in for added safety. "This is for someone from church. I'd like to run it by his house on our way home."

"No problem," Claire said as she started the car and headed for Little Rock with her reluctant passenger.

When they arrived in front of the Doctors' Building adjacent to St. Bernadette's, Claire helped Mrs. Lola Faye from the car and up the sidewalk.

"Mrs. Lola Faye, don't you think you need to use your cane?" Claire noticed the cane was tucked firmly under her companion's arm.

"Nope," Mrs. Lola Faye answered. There was a hint of defiance in the way she lifted her chin slightly. Claire surmised her friend was carrying the cane just to show people she didn't need its assistance.

Claire slowed her usually brisk pace to accommodate Mrs. Lola Faye. "This cane is awful handy," she commented as they crept toward the building. "I wrap it in rags and use it to dust the ceiling fans."

"I'd never have thought of that," Claire answered, gently steadying Mrs. Lola Faye as they stepped up onto the sidewalk.

"Oh, yeah. It's also good to drag jars from the back of the pantry."

As they approached the automatic sliding doors, Mrs. Lola Faye stopped short and waved the cane around in front of her. The doors obediently opened, and she nodded approvingly at the new employment she'd found for her little wooden friend.

When they entered the waiting room, Claire discovered Mrs. Lola Faye's favorite use for her cane.

"I tell you there's really no sense in *whack* this *whack* trip *Whack!* We could've been in a wreck with some of those maniac drivers and died for no good reason at all, because I'm telling you, I'm fine!" Here Mrs. Lola Faye violently struck the bell on the receptionist's desk with the head of the cane. The resulting jangle was so loud people all around the waiting room looked up in dismay. The receptionist herself only glanced up dully and handed Mrs. Lola Faye the sign-in sheet. "Please take a seat. The doctor will see you shortly," she said in a monotone voice.

"Fat chance," Mrs. Lola Faye snorted under her breath. The ride to the hospital had set her nerves on edge.

They settled into the vinyl waiting room chairs.

Mrs. Lola Faye picked up a magazine, pointed to the headline and said, "Don't imagine I need to read this anymore." The lurid pink lettering read "Seven Ways to Seduce Your Man Tonight." Mrs. Lola Faye tossed the magazine down and studied Claire, who had barely cracked a smile.

"Claire, something's on your mind. Now, you know you can tell me what's bothering you," she said softly. "So, if you want to talk about it, go right ahead." She waited, eyebrows raised expectantly, cane tapping rhythmically on Claire's shoe.

Claire dropped her shoulders in defeat. There was no sense fighting it. Between Gran and Mrs. Lola Faye, it seemed that strong-willed Southern matriarchs intent on helping her, whether she wanted it or not, were her lot in life. If she were truly honest with herself, she wasn't entirely sure she didn't want some advice.

She tried to choose her words carefully. "Have you ever wanted to do something, and worked for it, and waited for it, and then when it's almost time to do it, you just weren't sure anymore?"

Mrs. Lola Faye leaned her head back against the wall and closed her eyes. "Is this about a man?"

"No!" said Claire, too quickly. "I was talking about a job opening in Dallas. Remember when we first met in the hospital, and I told you how I'd always wanted to live and work in a big city?" She explained her interview dilemma and her mixed feelings as Mrs. Lola Faye listened. "And now I just don't know what I want or think or feel or anything." She heaved a gusty sigh and waited.

Mrs. Lola Faye cleared her throat in preparation for delivering her pearls of wisdom.

"Well now, I don't know nothing about that kind of thing. I always worked on the farm with Bud. Didn't have outside jobs, and I certainly didn't ever want to go anywhere off from here. But I do know what you mean about wanting something for so long and then not being sure."

Claire leaned forward expectantly. "I loved Bud Nugent from the minute I saw him and I wanted that man for my own. Man!" She chuckled under her breath. "We were just kids. But I didn't care and neither did he. My daddy and momma were a different story, though. I was their baby girl, after all. We both knew they weren't big on us gettin' married. I was underage, and I didn't figure they'd sign for me. So, one night Bud borrowed a car from somebody, Lord knows he couldn't afford his own, and we went to Louisiana. Down there I was legal to get married. That was what I'd been dreamin' about every day and night since we'd met."

She drew a deep breath and continued, "But when we got there and stood in front of the Justice of the Peace, I just froze. Couldn't say anything. Truth be told, I thought if I opened my mouth, I might throw up." She laughed, unscrewed the lid of her Mason jar, and took a drink. As she tightened it back in place, she continued.

"So the Justice of the Peace had got all the way to the

part where I was supposed to say 'I do.' That's all I had to say and it would be a done deal. But I just couldn't say it. I knew Momma and Daddy would be so disappointed and I started thinking I was too young and we were too poor and everything else you could think of." She began twisting her wedding band, worn thin from years of wear.

"Then how did you know you were doing the right thing?"

Mrs. Lola Faye gave her a wise smile. "I didn't."

Claire blinked in disbelief. "What?"

"I didn't know how it all would turn out. I *was* awful young and we *were* very poor. You can bet Momma and Daddy were upset, at first, anyway. But when I looked at Bud, looking at me and smiling that big ol' smile, next thing I knew the words were coming out of my mouth. Sometimes you don't know what you're gonna do 'til it's done. Then you just have to trust the Lord to help you. We were happy most of the time, that's for sure." To emphasize her point, she gave the chair next to her a thorough caning. *Whack!*

Claire blinked, slightly dumbfounded. This was the worst advice, or non-advice, she'd ever been given. "But, aren't you supposed to find peace with your decisions to know they're right?"

"Sure," said Mrs. Lola Faye thoughtfully. "But sometimes, you think you're at peace, then you're not, then you are, then you're not. See? So, I just looked at Bud and I guess *something* in me knew it was right. Maybe that was the Lord's doing."

"Lola Faye Nugent," called a stout nurse in green scrubs.

Mrs. Lola Faye hooked her cane over her arm. "No tellin' how long I'll be back here. They leave you in those rooms forever and a day." She followed the nurse through the door to the examination rooms, leaving Claire in stunned silence.

Flipping through back issues of *Arthritis Today* and *The AARP Journal* wasn't helping Claire quiet her mind, so she decided to take a walk.

Outside the waiting room, an orange Exit sign pointed to the right. Following it led to a narrow hallway and a flight of stairs with a "To Breezeway" sign next to them. Claire hadn't realized she was so close to the covered sidewalk that passed from Doctors' Buildings into the hospital.

I'll go see Rita and tell her about my interview. Claire was looking for a good pep talk, someone to tell her just how talented she was and what a bright future lay ahead of her. Frankly, she wasn't very sure of either at the moment.

She stumped up the stairs as quickly as she could, passing landing after landing until she came to the door that read "To Hospital." Shoving it open, Claire stepped into the glass covered walkway that connected the buildings of the medical compound. She slowed her pace and watched the people hurrying along below her. Some entered the hospital eagerly, as if they were excited to be there. She decided these were the ones going to see new babies in the family or to take loved ones home. Others walked slowly, with heads bent and eyes on the gray concrete. She didn't want to think what they were going to face down the long, cold hallways. She remembered trips like that when her mother was nearing the end. Claire stopped, and laid her head against the glass, feeling its cool pressure against her skin. She allowed herself to stay there only a few seconds, then headed off with a grim and determined set to her jaw.

When she entered the hospital, she knew at once she was on the wrong floor. She found the elevator and spent the short ride to the fifth floor looking into its mirrored walls at her muted reflection. Claire thought she looked tired and somehow old in the fingerprint-smudged metal door. It slid open with a ding and she exited, turning to the left.

Directly in front of her was an information desk. The hallway she needed was several doors down past this desk. Eyes on the floor, deep in thought, Claire had taken three or four steps off the elevator when she heard a sugary-sweet and alarmingly familiar voice. As the elevator door dinged shut behind her, Miranda Davenport said, "Ma'am, excuse me. Could you help me?"

Claire's head shot up. She was ten feet at most from the nurses' station where Miranda leaned with an easy grace, her back to Claire. She'd have recognized the voice anyway, even without the glossy chestnut hair and perfect feminine shape.

The nurse looked up from her paperwork without any particular concern and said, "What do you need?"

Her lack of enthusiasm must have annoyed Miranda,

whose voice seemed to stiffen and grow just a tad sweeter as she said, "Could you check the visitor's log for me? I'm meeting someone for lunch in the cafeteria and I need to know if he's here yet."

The nurse spun her chair toward the computer and said, "Name, please."

"Jake Weston. Reverend Jake Weston, actually. He's a pastor. I'm sure you've seen him here often. He comes to visit sick church members quite regularly." She talked about him, said his name and described him, with the relish of a hunter telling the story of the latest big kill.

Claire would've been sickened by it all if she'd not been desperate to get out of sight. She noticed a waiting room directly across from the nurses' desk.

Lord, I know you've got a lot more to deal with than this little drama, but please, help a girl out. Please get me out of here without Miranda seeing me. Amen. Claire edged over to the wall. Maybe she could sink through it if she tried hard enough. Walking quickly, with her head down, she made it into the waiting area without being spotted. Miranda was still tapping her blood-red manicured nails on the desk.

Thank you, God. I won't ask about something this petty ever again. Probably. Claire flung herself into a chair and grabbed the first book she saw. Her intention was to bury her face in it, just in case Miranda might come in the room and spot her. She couldn't hear what the nurse said, but in a minute Miranda's high-heeled sandals clicked away down the hall.

Claire's mind was whirling with anger, hurt, and more than a little jealousy. How could he? How could he meet Miranda for lunch? After that ride together in the woods. He'd taken her to the stream with the Jessamine and told her about the poem. Just because she'd said she wasn't interested didn't mean he could take up with that awful woman. Tears welled up in her eyes. Yes, it did. He was free to see anyone he liked. She'd turned him down. But Miranda?! Miranda Davenport, the closest thing to evil incarnate she could think of at the moment.

She was so furious it took her a while to notice the book she'd picked up. It was a children's book, hard-bound, with a bright yellow duck on the cover. The duck stood with its wings bent in an attitude that looked like an angry person with her hands on her hips. It was stomping a webbed foot in a puddle of water and, since the illustrator had given the animal eyebrows, one might even say the duck was frowning. This was a duck Claire could identify with.

"Maggie Puddlewaddle's Bad Mood," she read. Then underneath in smaller letters, "By Sage Finley."

This author has the same name as the Sage at church, Claire turned the book over, opening to the back inside cover. There, smiling back, was a picture of Dogwood's own Sage Finley. The author information read:

"Sage Finley lives on a farm in rural Arkansas with husband, daughters, and all kinds of animals who have inspired this series." Below was a list of books with titles like "Henrietta Hoppinpuff-Hare's Selfish Mood" and "Celsey Van DeCorn, The Saddest Cow."

I guess she did have some stories to tell. But she didn't have time to think about Sage, or unhappy cows, or stingy bunnies. She had to get back to the waiting room to pick up Mrs. Lola Faye and she had to do so without being detected by Miranda, whom she was beginning to think of as her archenemy. Maybe that description was a little overly dramatic. Still, if the stiletto-heeled shoe fit.

Claire crept stealthily back to the elevator and leaned against its wall as she descended back to the second floor. At least this settled whether or not she'd take the interview. She'd been a fool to even consider not going!

Back in the safety of the waiting room, Claire tried to pour all her attention into an article on how to crochet an afghan and was pretending to be deeply absorbed in her reading when Mrs. Lola Faye came back.

"Well, what did the doctor say? Is everything alright?" she asked, rising to leave.

"Fit as a fiddle. Just like I told you. Wasted trip. Didn't learn a thing new."

Lucky you, Claire thought as she and Mrs. Lola Faye left through the automatic doors, which opened effortlessly with a wave of the ever-useful cane.

Chapter Ten

They were almost back to Dogwood when Claire remembered that the flower riding in Mrs. Lola Faye's lap needed to be dropped off at its new home, wherever that was. She considered not mentioning it in hopes her passenger would forget it was there, but thought better of it.

"Mrs. Lola Faye, where are we taking that marigold?"

"I'm taking it to Joshua Hightower. You know, he lives on my old place. When I taught his Sunday school class last week, we learned about God making the plants in the Garden of Eden, and how Adam was supposed to tend to them. Joshua said he had a garden, but the bugs was eatin' his tomatoes. So I told Joshua I used to grow tomatoes and we always put a few marigolds out in between them because they keep the bugs away. I didn't know little boys had gardens anymore. Most of 'em sit and stare at the TV or the computer or something, I figure." She snorted disdainfully, then continued. "My Jesse was an outdoorsy one from the start. You couldn't make him sit still long enough to watch a whole movie hardly," she said with obvious pride. "So, I told Joshua I'd bring him a marigold next time I got out. I've also been wanting to see the place again. It's like visitin' a long lost friend every time I start up that driveway."

Claire swallowed as she considered how to ask the question that was rolling around in her mind without sounding nosy or gossipy. "I guess you've met Joshua's mom?"

The old lady's thin eyebrows knitted together. "Deloris? Yes, I've met her. She's a different sort of bird, isn't she? I can't quite make her out. Sometimes she kinda stares a hole in me, like you do when you see someone you think you recognize and you're trying to figure out where you know 'em from. But I'd never laid eyes on her in my life 'til the day she showed up wanting to look at the house."

Mrs. Lola Faye considered for a moment, then added,

"But she's not from these parts. Maybe people are just different wherever she's from. Colorado or South Dakota or somewhere off."

"I know it's none of my business, but do you know what happened to her? I mean, why she's in a wheelchair?"

Mrs. Lola Faye shook her head. "The talk was she had a car wreck some years back, but I don't know anything else. She's not one to just tell you her life story. I've asked her to church several times, and she always says she spends her time with Jesus at home, but thank you for inviting her." Then she asked curiously, "When have you met her?"

"I went with Paw to take Mr. Hightower a bull."

"Well, I bet you met Joshua then. Isn't he just the living end? I took a shine to him right from the get go."

They were turning into the long gravel drive by this time. Claire slowed the car to an easy pace as they bumped along through the dry mud holes. She could see Mrs. Lola Faye's face reflected in the passenger side window, looking out at the passing trees and smiling. She pointed out the edge of the property where the river lazed along under the summer sun.

"Jesse used to have a rope up in a tall pine over there. He'd swing out over the river and let go. I bet it was a twenty foot drop. Always a touch wild, that one."

Next she showed Claire where the old outhouse had once stood. "We used the Sears-Roebuck catalog for toilet paper. We didn't have the money to order anything, so we figured we might as well get some use out of them," Mrs. Lola Faye added merrily as they reached the house.

They stopped under a tall, spindly willow tree and stepped out of the car just in time to see Joshua swinging his way down from the uppermost branches.

"Mrs. Lola Faye! Miss Claire! Watch me," he called as he maneuvered through the leaves with reckless joy. The two women stared up at him. Claire had a look of horror on her face as she was sure the boy would fall at any moment.

Mrs. Lola Faye's expression was quite different. When Joshua finally swung from the lowest limb and landed at their feet, the old lady bent down and ruffled his hair. "That's some mighty good climbing. I used to have a little boy who liked to climb trees, too."

Joshua's eyes grew big, as if the thought of Mrs. Lola

Faye ever having a young child was more than he could imagine. Mrs. Lola Faye laughed and said, "You know, I haven't always been this old."

"You haven't?" he asked curiously.

"Joshua!!" His mother's sharp voice startled everyone. They all looked toward the front door, where Deloris was sitting, peering at them through the screen window. They'd been watching Joshua so intently, neither Claire nor Mrs. Lola Faye had noticed Deloris was silently observing them.

"I apologize for Joshua, Mrs. Nugent. He wasn't trying to be rude."

Mrs. Lola Faye cut her off with a warm laugh as she started up the porch steps. Claire held onto her elbow and helped her as they climbed. She wondered if Deloris would come onto the porch to speak with them today or if they'd have to conduct this visit through the screen door, as if they were visiting a prison inmate. To her surprise, Deloris opened the door and invited them in.

Mrs. Lola Faye looked around the small living room as they entered. She settled onto a sofa and said, "The place looks just lovely, Ms. Hightower. I really like this floral wallpaper you've put up. I've always been so fond of flowers."

Deloris said thank you, looked around at the rose-strewn wallpaper and then turned her eyes to the marigold perched on Mrs. Lola Faye's lap.

Mrs. Lola Faye followed her gaze and chuckled. "Yes, I like flowers so well I never leave home without one. This here is one of my favorite traveling companions. I just keep Claire around to drive for me." Mrs. Lola Faye was in rare form today.

Claire glanced at Mrs. Lola Faye. She continued to giggle, overcome by her own wit. She wondered how Deloris would take this silliness, but she was again surprised by her reaction.

Deloris was smiling, not a tense closed-lip smile, but a genuine toothy grin. And then, wonder of wonders, she started to laugh, quietly and under her breath, but laugh nonetheless. Claire stared at the two in utter amazement. Joshua, who had followed them in and plopped down on the sofa next to Mrs. Lola Faye, was equally mystified at his mother's reaction. He looked at Claire and gave a slight shrug of his skinny shoulders.

By this time, Mrs. Lola Faye had regained her composure. She lifted her glasses, wiped her eyes, and said, "Oh, really, Ms. Hightower, I came to give Joshua this marigold for his garden. He told me at church the other Sunday that the bugs were eating his tomatoes up. So I said I'd bring him something to help with that little problem. Would it be alright if I took him out back and showed him how to plant it? Won't take but a minute. I'd sure love to see the old garden again, all greened up and doin' good."

Deloris shifted uneasily in her chair. After a moment of deliberation, she hesitantly agreed. As the two left to test out their green thumbs, Claire glanced nervously around her. The only noise was the tick-tock of a grandfather clock that stood against the far wall. Deloris sat smoothing out the front of her blouse and picking invisible lint from her pants legs. The clock struck the hour with a resounding gong-gong-gong, so abrupt and loud that Claire jumped. Deloris didn't acknowledge it and continued sitting in disconcerting quiet. At last, she looked at Claire and said, "So, are you and Mrs. Nugent close?"

Claire didn't really know how to explain their fast friendship, and frankly she thought it was rather an odd thing for Deloris to ask.

"Mrs. Lola Faye was a patient of mine at St. Bernadette's. Then I found out she went to Dogwood church and we just hit it off. She's an exceptional lady. I think she kind of adopted me when we were in the hospital. She's needed some help keeping house lately, so I've been lending a hand. "

Claire couldn't really come up with a good way to tell Deloris why she'd become so attached to Mrs. Lola Faye in such a short amount of time. But she tried, piling words upon words, never really getting much said. Deloris sat and listened intently as Claire talked on.

"I guess Mrs. Lola Faye is just one of those people you can't help but love, even when you first meet them," Clare finished.

Deloris nodded. "I've met a few like that myself. They just come along and bring sunshine with them, don't they?" She smiled to herself, and Claire felt again that she was an intruder into some very private part of Deloris's past.

Just to have something to say, Claire added, "She

doesn't have any family close by. Her only child lives in Mountain View, and they don't get to see each other much."

Deloris's eyes darted to meet Claire's. There was an almost hungry look in them. "Does she say much about him?"

Claire was taken aback. She wondered how Deloris knew Mrs. Lola Faye had a son, especially since she'd only said "child."

Before she could answer, Joshua and Mrs. Lola Faye came back. The knees of Joshua's jeans were muddy, and Claire noticed Mrs. Lola Faye's stockings were in the same sorry condition.

"Well, we got 'em planted!" said Joshua, wiping his hands on his shirt with satisfaction.

"Now, if you need some more, you just let me know," Mrs. Lola Faye said as she headed toward the front door. To Deloris she added, "I won't take anymore of your time. Thank you for letting me come in and visit with my old home for a minute. I made some wonderful memories here. I hope you and yours will, too."

Deloris thanked her for the marigold and followed them onto the porch. She watched Claire help Mrs. Lola Faye down the steps, gently chiding her for crawling around on the ground.

"Well, I better get used to having dirt on me. I'll have about six feet of it on me before too much longer!"

"Mrs. Lola Faye! Don't even joke about that," Claire scolded.

****

With Mrs. Lola Faye safely deposited in her trailer house and the day's adventures over, Claire finally had a few moments to think. She washed the supper dishes for Gran and looked out the little window above the sink. *What was going on with Deloris Hightower? Why was she so interested in Mrs. Lola Faye? And more importantly, what was the deal with Miranda and Jake?*

She wrinkled her nose in disgust and wiped a soapy hand across her brow. It didn't matter, she reminded herself quickly. She'd schedule the interview in the morning and, if all went well, that would be the end of all this rigmarole.

The next morning, Claire called and spoke with Mr. Jasper Johnson, Nurse Recruiter for Dallas Presbyterian

Hospital. He seemed eager to meet with her in person as soon as possible.

"Would this Thursday be feasible for you?" he asked in a clipped, businesslike voice. Claire tried to sound equally professional and not too eager as she said, "That would be just fine."

The appointment was set. She would meet Mr. Johnson the very next day. She hung up the phone and collapsed wearily onto a kitchen chair. It was only nine in the morning, but she already felt like she needed a nap. And worst of all, she realized, it was Wednesday. Gran attended a Ladies' Bible Study at the church on Wednesday nights, and she wanted Claire to come along. It just so happened the parsonage was attached to the church by a very short sidewalk. She banged her head gently on the table.

Claire felt a wave of relief rush over her when she saw Jake's truck wasn't at home as they walked into the Fellowship Hall for Bible Study that night. Then a sick feeling followed as she wondered if he was out with Miranda. *I'm going to have to start wearing a rubber band on my wrist and just pop the fire out of myself when I think things like that.*

She settled into a metal folding chair next to Gran. It was almost seven o'clock, time for the class to start, but no teacher stood behind the podium.

"Gran, who teaches this class?" Claire asked.

"Sage Finley," Gran replied. "She's always just about late. Got two little kids and I'm just amazed she ever gets anywhere or gets anything done. But she's a good teacher and thinks a lot about the things of the faith."

At two minutes until seven, Sage came bustling in the side door. Her hair was slipping out of her ponytail holder and she was balancing several books, a Bible, and a plate of cookies.

"Sorry, y'all. I forgot it was my night to do refreshments until I was walking out the door." She slid a plate of Oreos onto the counter and said seriously, "Fresh out of the oven. Now, are we all here?" A quick head count showed all eight women were indeed present, with the addition of Claire. Sage scooted her podium closer to the semi-circle of folding chairs and said, "OK, let's get started."

The lesson was one in a series on the apostles, and

tonight's man of the hour was John. Sage talked about John's fiery personality and the need for all kinds of different types of people in God's work. "John learned to value his relationship with Christ over the power and prestige that could come with being one of the chosen twelve," she added.

"I think," Sage said, biting the corner of her lower lip thoughtfully, "we tend to do a pretty bad job of defining success in relational terms, do you know what I mean?" There were several confused looks, so she continued. "What I mean is, we assess ourselves and our lives with 'what' instead of 'who.' What have I done in my career? What goals have I met and what's the next step in my plan? What did I accomplish today? Checking things off the list, basically. I don't think there's anything wrong with that, necessarily, but it's so easy to forget the *whos* in your life. Who do I love and serve and who loves me?"

There was a momentary pause in Sage's fast-paced speech, and Claire looked up to see Sage's eyes were filled with tears. She said, rather matter-of-factly, "Y'all know I make it a practice to cry at every single one of these lessons over something or other, so here's tonight's Kleenex moment." Someone handed her a tissue, and everyone, including Sage, laughed as she continued.

"I went through a time when I felt like nothing I did mattered. At the end of the day I'd look around and say, what did I do today? Well, I changed four dirty diapers, cleaned up three spilled milks, wiped runny noses and then wiped them some more, fixed some meals and cleaned up the dishes, washed clothes, folded them and put them up. Everything I'd done would be undone in just a few minutes. None of it was exactly scrapbook material, you know? And it just seemed like my world was so small."

"Then, one day, I was outside watching the girls play and thinking of what I was going to cook for supper and it just hit me. I can do all these things out of a sense of obligation, because I *have* to, or I can do them because I *love* the people I'm doing them for."

She looked around at the faces of the women, a small group of students in a small country church, and continued, "Lots of things seem like they don't amount to much when we use our perspective, but when you try to think of them as

God does, it all changes. We read about these heroes of the faith, like John, who did great things for God. We consider them great mainly because they affected lots of people and they're well-known. But whoever said God cared about numbers or name recognition? One heart matters as much to God as a hundred or a hundred thousand. Who knows how many saints served the Lord at the same time as the apostles, lived faithfully, loved greatly, and then went to their reward, leaving just a handful of people who remembered them. God remembers them and He remembers us. The more I think about it, the more I believe that in His eyes, love is everything. Love God, love people, show it in your life. Because if you don't have that, well, like Paul said, you're nothing."

As Sage closed in prayer, Claire bowed her head and closed one eye. With the other, she stole a glance at Gran, who was fervently praying along with Sage, her lips moving as silent words ascended from her heart to Heaven. She felt privileged to be sitting there beside a woman who had lived her life well, quietly working and serving God in her own little corner of the world. True, she filled that corner with lots of unsolicited advice, but she loved the people God brought into her life. Loved them mightily. Claire slipped her hand into Gran's, and gave it a gentle squeeze.

"Amen," Sage concluded. They all stood up, stretched, complained about needing to get some cushions for those chairs, and began to drift over to the kitchen area.

Sage approached Claire, who was eating an Oreo and wishing she had a glass of milk. "Hey, Claire! I'm so glad you could come tonight. I hope I didn't preach at you too much. I get a little carried away sometimes, I think." Claire assured her she'd enjoyed the class, then ventured the question that had been in her mind the entire evening.

"Sage, I saw some of your books yesterday. I didn't know you were a writer. How did that happen?"

Sage laughed merrily and licked the filling of her cookie before she answered. "It all started during a day when I was feeling sorry for myself, which happens more often than I care to admit. If I remember right, it was while I was getting ketchup out of one of the girl's hair. I was thinking how I'd always wanted to be a writer and how I'd probably never get to do it now because I was so busy with the kids. It was a great pity party until God tapped me on the head and said, 'So quit whining and be a writer if that's what you want.' I started making excuses and He said, 'All you have to do to be a writer is write.'"

She leaned forward and said seriously, "God has to talk pretty plain to me sometimes. I'd been thinking I needed a full-job at some magazine or a newspaper to be a *real* writer, whatever that meant. Something with a desk and regular hours and all that. But really, I just needed to write because I loved it and it made me happy. I think when we use the gifts God's given us with joy, it brings Him joy." She touched Claire's shoulder, a habit she had when talking with anyone, then added, "That's just Sage-theology. Anyway, even if nobody ever read it except my kids and my husband, I enjoyed the writing process, you know?"

Claire nodded; Sage went on. "I started writing down the stories I told my girls at bedtime. I wrote at night mostly, after they were asleep. Then, just to see what would happen, I sent one off to a publisher and here I am."

"Does anyone at church know you've had all these books published?" Claire asked.

"Oh, I don't know. I've mentioned it to a few people, but I don't make it a regular topic of conversation. I know I've talked about it before in Bible study, because it was the best personal example I had of being content with circumstances while also trying to make the most of them." Sage shifted gears as easily as she talked, and almost as rapidly. "So, how's your job search going?"

Claire told her about the interview, and Sage was predictably enthusiastic. "I think nursing is a great profession. You can really feel like you've changed someone's life for the better and helped them when they needed it with a job like that."

"Ever since I was a little girl, I've wanted to do this." Claire replied, recalling her motive truly had been just that good-hearted at one time. She realized it had changed as she grew older.

She looked at Sage, who was now chatting with the other ladies as if they were her own sisters. While all the other women sipped coffee, Sage went to the refrigerator and pulled out a jug of milk. She poured some into a coffee mug and began dunking her Oreos with a look of complete satisfaction on her face.

****

Gran and Claire arrived home to find Paw sleeping soundly in the recliner. "I don't know why he won't just go to bed. This always puts a crick in his neck," Gran fussed as she and Claire sat down on the slip-covered sofa. Claire settled back and stared up at the ceiling tiles while Gran scanned the television listings.

"Nothing on, as usual. TV's nothing but trash these days, really. Only thing decent is 'Wheel of Fortune.'"

Gran stood slowly, yawned, and moved to Paw's chair to wake him. "We better get to bed. Us old folks can't handle late nights 'cause we always get up at 5:00 in the morning, no matter what time we go to bed. Couldn't stay awake if we tried, anyway. Might as well turn in now." She stopped and said gently, "You better hit the hay too, girl. Got a big day ahead of you tomorrow."

Claire nodded, kissed Gran's wrinkled cheek, and went to bed but found sleep wouldn't come. She lay awake, thinking of her family, of Sage, and of God and His love.

An odd idea spun through her mind in the midst of all the other whirling thoughts. Claire wished she were the kind of person who would feel comfortable dunking her cookies in milk while everyone else primly sipped their coffee. She turned over and gave her pillow a sound punching.

I'd be worried about what other people thought and drink the coffee because everyone else was.

She continued lying there, trying to stop looking at the clock.

I don't even like coffee.

Her mind finally slowed and thoughts began to blur into dreams.

Jake Weston would eat his Oreos with milk...and enjoy every bite.

A faint smile touched her lips as she faded into sleep.

Chapter Eleven

Claire reflected on the interview, which had gone well for the most part, as she drove back toward Dogwood. Her thoughts were moving fast, as was the traffic. She tried to keep her mind on it, watching out for the drivers who felt brakes were optional and that frequent and sudden lane changes were necessary.

Mr. Johnson had been friendly in a practiced, professional way. He'd mentioned Rita Sparks' referral in glowing terms and made small talk about how she was doing now and asked if Claire had enjoyed being in Rita's classes. He had asked all the typical questions. Where did she expect to be in five years? What were her greatest strengths and weaknesses? What were her professional goals?

The last one was the only one she hadn't been prepared for, although she should have seen it coming. For every other question, she'd given the poised and carefully constructed answer she'd spent the drive to Dallas rehearsing over and over in her mind and out loud to the steering wheel. After all of those, Jasper had lifted his eyes from the notebook, tapped his pen on the desk and said, "What originally drew you to the profession of nursing?"

"My mom," Claire had replied without an instant of hesitation. Jasper Johnson raised one eyebrow in inquiry, and Claire had immediately launched into the story of that long ago trip to a hospital obstetrics floor and her mother's comments as they stood watching the nurses work. She heard herself telling him about her experiences with nurses while her mother had been ill, and how much she'd wanted to help others, like they did.

Mr. Johnson had scratched his black mustache with the end of his pen, then leaned forward and rested his elbows on the polished, massive desk. Claire's head was swimming, dizzied by the sudden flood of emotion that came with those long ago memories. She felt she'd said far too much about her personal life.

Mr. Johnson's voice had sounded like it came from a mile away when he'd said, "I'm sure you realize, Ms. Burke, that you're applying for a floor nurse position at this time. But, should you be hired, there will likely be an OB position open in the future."

I came across as overly sentimental and gushing. Why do I have to ramble so much? She frowned and tightened her grip on the steering wheel.

Everything after that had gone smoothly, though. There were other candidates to interview, but Mr. Johnson had said he really enjoyed talking with Claire and would let her know something by the middle of next week at the latest.

After berating herself for her unfocused blabbering, Claire worried for a while that at times she'd sounded too polished.

Maybe I didn't come off like a beauty pageant contestant. Her eyes narrowed as thoughts of Miranda swarmed through her mind like pestering horseflies. And thoughts of Jake, of course. Always Jake.

Claire rolled her eyes. Everything was so annoying. Aggravating. Worrisome. She'd be glad when it was over. At least she'd know soon what her next move should be, whether it was accepting the position at Dallas Presbyterian or starting the search again.

The sun was beginning to sink over the pines when Claire made it back home. The sky was an odd blend of orange and deep, glowing rose pink that she could only remember seeing at her grandparents' place. Claire stopped on the porch and watched its slow descent as the evening faded into twilight purple.

Paw looked up from his whittling as she entered.

"Whatcha makin'?" she asked, settling into the couch, watching wood shavings curl under Paw's knife and drop onto the newspaper spread under his feet.

Paw turned the piece of cedar thoughtfully, considering it from every angle. "Don't know yet. It'll have to decide what it wants to be."

Gran came in and plopped down next to Claire. "We ate without you. You know how your Paw gets when his supper is late."

Paw shaved a curl of wood from the block and said,

without looking up, "Don't you blame it on me, Millie. You were hungry, too."

"Well, fine," Gran admitted. "It just sounds better to say it was you. After all, ladies should have delicate appetites."

Paw let out a snorting laugh. "Ain't nothing delicate about you, Millie Burke."

Gran fixed him in an indignant stare. "I have very delicate feelings, Franklin." She faked a look of extreme hurt before saying to Claire. "I left you a plate on the table. Everything's still warm."

Claire was thoroughly enjoying her pork chops when Gran came in and sat down beside her. From the way she kept pursing her lips, Claire knew she was trying to decide how to tell her something.

"Spit it out, Gran," she said, laying down a fork still laden with black-eyed peas.

"Jake called for you." It was the first time Claire could recall Gran referring to him by his first name alone.

"And?"

"He said he needs your help with something. I told him you'd be back tonight. He's going to call back later."

As if on cue, the phone rang.

Claire looked at it, looked at Gran, and didn't budge. Gran sighed and moved to the phone.

"Hello? Yes, she's back. I'll get her."

Claire frowned and reluctantly sat down at the old roll-top desk where the only rotary phone still in use in the county waited for her.

"Hello?" she said, trying to sound as if she were speaking to a telemarketer or some other stranger with whom she had no personal connection.

"Claire, how are you?" Jake asked. He sounded distracted, preoccupied. Claire was sure he wasn't really listening or he would've noticed the reserved coolness of her answer. "I'm fine."

"Listen," Jake rushed on, "I just had a strange phone call from Deloris Hightower. She says she needs me to come over to her house...tonight, if possible. She wants you to come, too."

"What?" Claire forgot her anger at Jake. "Why?"

"I don't know, but she was very insistent. I know it's getting late, but I really feel like we should do this as soon as we can."

"Did she sound upset?" Claire asked.

"No. Just the opposite. She was very calm. She says she needs to tell us something."

Claire glanced at Gran, who was turning off the TV and trying to nudge Paw awake. They would both be turning in for the night soon.

"Please help me with this, Claire. I've spent a lot of time visiting with Deloris, and this is the first time she's ever specifically asked me to come talk with her. I've had a feeling she needed to get something off her chest for awhile now. It might really help her." His voiced trailed off.

Claire hesitated, "OK. I'll meet you there."

"I'm leaving now. Good-bye." There was a pause. "Thank you, Claire," Jake added as he hung up.

She replaced the receiver. *Did that phone call really just happen?*

"Gran, I'll be back in a little while." Paw shuffled by with Gran at his heels. Gran kissed her granddaughter's forehead and mercifully went to bed without another word.

Claire stepped out into the humid night air. The sky was now black and starless as she hurried to her car on a path lit only by the dim glow of the porch light's bare bulb.

The long gravel drive that led to Deloris's house seemed endless as Claire crept along. She kept an alert watch for the deer Mrs. Lola Faye had warned her lived on the land. According to her elderly friend, deer were prone to jump out in front of a car at night, confused by the oncoming lights. Claire saw their eyes shining from the tall grass by the lane, but thankfully they retreated deeper into the fields instead of dashing out into her path.

Please let Jake be here already. As Claire approached the house, she felt a wave of relief when her headlights shone on the beat-up tailgate of Jake's truck.

He was sitting in the driver's seat, head bowed, praying. As she turned off her car, Jake lifted his head and climbed out. He started towards her. "Ready?" he asked.

"It would help to know what I'm supposed to be ready for," Claire replied as Jake knocked on the front door.

The house was dark except for the living room where Deloris waited for them. She was not in her wheelchair tonight. Instead she reclined on the sofa, chin in hand. Her golden eyes were fixed intently on the front door as her visitors entered.

"Brother Weston, Ms. Burke," Deloris began, "I apologize for the late hour. I wanted to do this while William and Joshua were away. I've sent them into town to see a movie. Thank you so much for coming." She was collected and steady, but there was an odd intensity in her voice.

"I have a favor to ask you, both of you."

Claire and Jake settled into armchairs opposite Deloris as she continued speaking.

"I pride myself on not asking for help often, but there's something I feel must be done and now is the time."

Jake leaned forward, elbows on his knees, "I'll do anything I can, Deloris." Claire was looking into the swirling colors of the large braided rug that separated them from where Deloris sat. In the silence that followed Jake's words, she knew she should offer the same sentiment. No words would come out. She glanced at Deloris, who was absently running a finger across the scar that marred the skin of her neck. Claire cut her eyes at Jake. He was patiently waiting for Deloris to continue.

Slowly, she began again. "I need to explain some things first." She swallowed hard and inhaled slowly.

"Before I came here, I was a different woman. I had what is sometimes called a 'substance abuse' problem. I've told you as much before, Brother Weston." An eerie half-smile tilted her lips, one of the saddest expressions Claire had ever seen. "It was just a chance for me to do the abusing for a change," she added in a hollow tone, almost as an afterthought.

Her eyes met Claire's and she waved her thin hand. "I don't want to make excuses for the things I did, for hurting the people I hurt. I just want the two of you to understand how I could do what I did." She seemed to steel herself. Claire and Jake waited.

"I met a man," Deloris continued. "A gentle, caring man, the kind who laughed as easily as most people draw breath. He told the most wonderful stories, about his childhood and the place he came from. He could make anyone feel like they'd known him forever."

A genuine smile flickered and lit her face for a brief second, then died away. "I still have no idea what he saw in me. Maybe he wanted to help me. I hid so much from him at first. He had no idea what he was getting tangled up in."

She shook her head and began rubbing her forehead. Her eyelids drooped. The lamp light shone on her down-turned face and Claire thought she'd never seen anyone look quite so tired.

"He lost someone he loved not long after we started seeing each other. That's when the depression started. He told me once he could remember being happy, *knew* in his head that he had been happy before. But he couldn't remember what it *felt* like."

"We started going out to bars. Local honkytonks, places like that. It was what I did to make myself feel better. I thought it would help him, too. Alcohol takes care of all kinds of memories. For a while, anyway. I moved on to harder things. I'm so thankful he never did."

She stopped again and looked intently at Jake. "I know it sounds crazy to you, and it does to me now, too, but I really thought I was helping him the whole time I was dragging him down. It started just on the weekends. We'd do anything we could think of that was crazy and sounded like fun."

Deloris leaned over to the end table beside the sofa and pulled open a drawer. She took out a thin gold band and rolled it slowly between her thumb and forefinger. "One weekend, we decided to get married."

"I did love him," she said sharply, meeting both their eyes for the first time. "You have to believe that. As much as someone in that shape can love anyone." She was almost pleading with them. Claire nodded slowly, prompting Deloris to continue.

"Things went from bad to worse. When he realized the condition we were both in, he wanted us to get help. I didn't. He started going to church, like he had before. Tried to talk to me about God and what He wanted. What did I care? What had God ever done for me?"

"One night he came home and said he couldn't stand to see me like that anymore. He begged me to get into a treatment program with him."

A solitary tear slid down her cheek and fell onto the gold band cupped in her hand. "I told him to leave. To take his preaching and his God and just go. I said I never wanted to see him again. And I threw this at him." She lifted the ring, then let her hand fall limply to her lap.

"What'd he say?" Claire asked before she realized the words were coming.

"He picked up my ring and laid it on the table. I was sitting there with my glass of whatever it was that night. He told me he couldn't make me change and wouldn't try to force me, but he wouldn't stay where he wasn't wanted. He told me he loved me. And he walked out the door."

Deloris shifted uncomfortably on the couch. "I don't know how long I sat there, but sometime later...it was still dark, I remember that... I got in the car and started driving. I don't remember where I was going or anything about the wreck except hearing the wheels crunching on the gravel when I dropped off the edge of the road. That was right before I started to roll, I guess. The police said I flipped the car three times. I woke up in the hospital four weeks later and stayed there for another three months. I was a broken up mess, but that time in the hospital forced me to get clean and sober. It saved my life. And my son's life.

"You were carrying Joshua when all this happened?"

"I didn't know!" Deloris said quickly. "I want to believe I wouldn't have knowingly put my baby in danger, even as messed up as I was. The doctor's told me later I was only a couple of weeks along when the accident happened. When I left the hospital, I went straight to an inpatient treatment place. Run by a religious organization, if you can believe it." She smiled at Jake as she said this.

"I had a lot of time to think before I left there. I'd been given a second chance and I knew it. Plus I had someone else to live for now. When I got out, I called my brother and asked if he would come away with me and help me get settled somewhere else, just temporarily. It's been seven years and he can't tear himself away from Joshua. Or this place. I knew we'd love it here. I just knew it. When we drove up the lane and I saw this house, I felt like I was finally coming home."

"So, how did you end up here? Dogwood is a place you've really got to be looking for to find," Claire asked.

Jake leaned forward in his chair, a look of comprehension dawning on his face. He started to speak, but Deloris stopped him with a raised finger. She turned to

Claire and said, "I'd heard all about it from my husband. Jesse grew up here, in this house."

Chapter Twelve

The clock ticked, loud in the silent living room. Jake sank back in his chair and the springs squeaked softly. They were all very quiet as Deloris continued to hold Claire in her amber gaze, watching carefully, waiting for her reaction.

For a few long moments, Claire said nothing.

"Deloris," she began when she finally found her voice again, "are you telling me that you were...are, I guess...married to Jesse Nugent? Mrs. Lola Faye's son?"

Deloris nodded.

"So that means," Claire stopped as another implication became clear in her thoughts, "Joshua is..."

"Her grandson, yes." Deloris finished the sentence for Claire and hurried on. "She knew that Jesse was seeing someone in Montana, before his father died. But he always called me Lori. When he mentioned me in his letters or phone calls to his mother, it was always by that name. Just to make sure no one would figure out who I was when we moved here, I took my half-brother's last name. I went by Chidester before. So, even if Jesse had told his mother all about us, she would've known me as Lori Chidester."

Claire's jaws tightened and she felt a burning sensation rising in her throat. "Forgive me if I sound harsh, Deloris. Or Lori, or whatever you want to be called. You've been living here for at least seven years and are acquainted with Mrs. Lola Faye. You know she has no family close by, at least to *her* knowledge, and you know she lives alone. I'm sure you realize she's a kind, good woman. No one in Dogwood would argue with that. How have you justified keeping her only grandchild a secret all these years? A secret in the home she lived in for most of her life!"

Claire was clenching her fists tightly in her lap, and Jake glanced at her nervously. Her face was a deep red to rival the shade of her hair.

"Not to mention what you've kept from Jesse. You said

yourself he was a decent man until you got hold of him, and that he'd straightened himself up. But you've never told him he has a son, knowing how much family meant to him? I'm sorry, but that just seems wrong," Claire finished heatedly.

Deloris looked at Jake for help. "Brother Weston, we've talked many times before about forgiveness and redemption. At first, I was angry at Jesse for leaving me. I felt like he didn't want me and he wouldn't want our child. And even if he did, so what? That's how bitter I was. Later, after I began to see things more clearly, I could understand his point of view. He felt he had to get away from me and the mess we were together."

A solitary tear slipped down her face. "I was so ashamed of what I'd put him through. I knew it was wrong not to tell him about Joshua, but at the same time I kept thinking it wasn't fair to put such a burden on Jesse. He never asked for this."

She pointed to her wheelchair. "I'll never walk again. Not in this life, anyway, because of the bad choices I made. I did it to myself; I couldn't see asking him to take me back when I didn't feel like I was the woman he married anymore."

Their eyes met, and Claire saw Deloris's deep suffering etched on her striking face. "I know it was wrong. I understand that now and it's time for me to try to set things right. But I need your help. And yours," Deloris said, turning to Jake.

"Why?" Claire asked softly.

Deloris dropped her gaze, and almost whispered, "Jesse deserves the truth." She let out a shuddery sigh and continued. "But I'm not sure I can handle telling him myself. I don't know what he'd do if I showed up on his doorstep and said, 'Hello, just wanted to tell you we have a son.' But I think if someone he could respect and trust came to him first and tried to tell him what happened, then I could meet with him and explain why I did everything I did."

Jake stood and began pacing back and forth on the worn rug. He ran his fingers through his hair distractedly.

"Deloris, I understand, to a degree, why you would ask me to speak with Jesse. People often seek out pastors to help mend family differences."

She interrupted him, "Oh, but you're not just any

pastor. I know I don't come to your church services, but I listen to them every week and I've come to feel you're just as much my pastor as any one of your members. Besides that, I know Jesse will listen to you because you're a man of God and his mother's pastor. That's important and it will matter to him."

"Deloris, I'm not sure why you've brought Claire into this," Jake said. "The two of you barely know each other."

"That's true, but Mrs. Lola Faye adores Claire. I've seen them together. I think if Claire goes along with you, she can tell Jesse how much it would mean to his mother if he'd come home and try to make things work. Not with me, mind you. I'm not foolish enough to hope for that. I just pray he'll try to build a relationship with Joshua. Jesse will take the news better coming from you and Claire, since she and Mrs. Lola Faye are good friends. Do you see, Claire?" Deloris asked, almost desperately.

"Yes, I suppose," Claire ventured. "So, you want us to go to Jesse Nugent and tell him you're living in Dogwood, in his childhood home, and, oh by the way, you have his child? That's an awful lot to drop on a person you've just met."

"I know, I know," Deloris said hurriedly, "but it's so important that I try to make this right. If it doesn't happen now, I might lose my nerve again. I've tried to contact him several times. I called him on and off over the years, but I'd always hang up when he answered the phone. I even found his current address."

She pulled a tattered piece of paper from her pocket and held it out to Claire, who took it from her warily. "I don't drive anymore, not since the accident, and I don't want William to take me to find him. When I've mentioned it in the past, he's said to leave well enough alone and let the man live his life. He's always been against me contacting Jesse, and I don't want him to know until it's all said and done. I even considered writing a letter. I bet I've started a dozen over the years, but I never can get the words out right. I've never been good at getting things down on paper. They just don't come out right, and this is something that *has* to be handled well. That's why I'm asking you two for help." She held out her hands to them, hope glowing in her golden eyes.

Jake walked over and sat perched on the arm of Claire's

chair. "Well, Deloris, I certainly admire your desire to make amends with the people you've wronged in the past. I also agree Jesse and Mrs. Lola Faye would be a wonderful addition to Joshua's life, as he would be to theirs. But this is an awful lot to digest in one sitting. Can Claire and I talk this over tonight and get back with you in the morning?"

The grandfather clock began to toll. "That would be just fine. It's getting late and Joshua and William will be coming home soon. I don't want to rush you but...well, please just let me know as soon as you decide."

Jake crossed over to Deloris and squeezed her shoulder gently. "I'll pray about this tonight."

Claire stood slowly and nodded assent as she followed Jake out the front door.

****

The air still held a hint of the day's muggy heat as Jake and Claire sat on her grandparents' front step, an occasional beetle clinking off the light bulb that burned overhead. Jake had followed Claire back there so they could talk about what to do with Deloris's request, but for the moment they sat without speaking. The night was still. Even the crickets had gone to bed. Not a single oak leaf stirred, and the mockingbirds slept peacefully, quiet for once.

Jake was the first to speak. "Just so you know, not all my visits around the community are that...umm, revealing, I guess you could say. I usually spend a lot of time admiring people's gardens and talking about the weather. Or who's sick and with what."

One corner of Claire's mouth twitched into a feeble half-smile. "That's good. Otherwise, you'd be more talk-show host than minister."

Jake nodded. "I wish I could say this was the first story like that I've heard, though. You can't imagine the pain and heartbreak people carry around inside them while they're chatting with the neighbors or singing in the choir or whatever. Sometimes it has to come out, and I'm glad...well maybe not *glad*...more like honored to have gained people's respect in this community so they feel comfortable sharing their troubles with me."

He paused and rubbed the stubble on his chin. It made a soft rasping noise as he sat thinking for a long minute. "That's why I'm going to do this for Deloris. I prayed about it

100

on the way over here, and I think God is leading me to try and help her. Her intentions are sincerely good, I believe. She's just scared to take that first step. When a person wants to tell the truth and make amends, I think that's an honorable thing. So I'm going to find Jesse for her, if I can, and lay out the basic facts and encourage him to meet with Deloris and Joshua."

He met Claire's eyes. She'd been watching him as he talked, noticing the deep feeling in his voice and the determined set of his jaw. She could tell Jake Weston was on a mission.

"I understand if you don't want to do this with me, but, I'd really appreciate it if you came along."

Claire drew a deep breath, held it for a second, then blew it out forcefully. "When were you planning on leaving?"

"Monday morning, early."

She would go. *For Mrs. Lola Faye. It has nothing to with Jake and my feelings for him, whatever they were.*

"I'll do it for Mrs. Lola Faye. She has a right to know her grandson, but I agree Jesse needs to know first, then he can tell his mother. What time do you want to get started?"

"Seven all right?" he asked, barely suppressing a grin.

Claire nodded. Jake stood and stretched. "It's beautiful country, the northern part of the state."

He ambled down the sidewalk, hands shoved into the pockets of his jeans. When he reached the truck, he stopped. Claire could barely see his face in the darkness as he said, "This means a lot to me. It's nice not to have to do everything alone." He rapped his knuckles on the hood of his truck, filling the silence as he searched for words. "Well, see you in church Sunday." He bounded into the driver's seat. The engine grumbled to life and he was gone.

Claire closed her eyes and lay back on the concrete. It was cool against her tired, aching back. She lay there contemplating the long, eventful, exhausting day. *The sooner I hear from Dallas the better*, as she finally stirred herself enough to make it into the house.

****

Sunday morning found the Burkes in their usual pew. Paw sat on the end, his elbow on the back of the bench. Claire suspected Paw did this so he could casually lean over and rest his head on his hand if he felt sleepy. Paw attempted to nap in church regularly, but Gran was always waiting with a sharp left jab to the ribs to recall him to wakeful piety. What Claire found most amusing was the way Gran could inflict these merciless jabs without ever taking her eyes, full of serene attentiveness, off the pulpit. Paw would wake with a start and cut his eyes reproachfully at Gran, who would inevitably be engrossed in the day's message.

For the time being, everyone was fully awake as the choir sang their hearts out to get the Lord's Day started off right. The old shaped-note hymnals were battered from years of use and none of the singers really needed them to know the words.

The men's side of the choir had a bass lead. Claire smiled to herself as the men gave it their all to hit the low, low notes. They tucked their chins into their chests and looked an awful lot like linebackers as they growled out their part. Then it was the ladies' turn as the sopranos took over. Eyebrows were lifted and necks were stretched as the women strained for the high notes, creating a goose-like visual effect. The music itself was lovely, heartfelt and strong, a song called "I Don't Know About Tomorrow."

Many things about tomorrow
I don't seem to understand.
But I know who holds tomorrow
And I know who holds my hand.

The song had been requested by Jake to go along with his sermon for the day, a message on facing the future.

"You will have God's help when you need it, and not a moment sooner. Let Him deal with your future. You only have to deal with tomorrow as it becomes today," Jake concluded. Before dismissing them in prayer, he stepped down from behind the pulpit and said, "As always, please pray for each other and pray for your pastor as I try to minister to the needs of the people God brings my way."

Claire knew tomorrow's excursion was on his mind and his sermon about not worrying was preached as much for his own good as the congregation's.

Afterward, everyone stood outside chatting and squinting in the brilliant sunlight. This was what Jake called "the yard service," the time when the church body fellowshipped outside after the official meeting time was over. Claire always felt a little lost, moving through the clusters of conversation, trying to find a spot where she could join in.

A group of farmers, including Paw, discussed haying and such to her left, while some women talked about an upcoming wedding shower on her right. At last, she spotted Mrs. Lola Faye, huddled in deep conversation with Gran. She was headed in that direction when Jake finally emerged from the church, having stayed to shake the hand of every person in attendance.

He spotted Claire and started her way, only to be interrupted by Miranda. She stepped in his path as he wove between the groups of visiting people. Claire saw this little interception, and came to a sudden stop. She turned her back to Miranda and tried to appear a part of the bunch of women discussing so-and-so's new baby.

Claire strained to hear the conversation behind her. "Brother Jake, I just wanted to thank you again for having lunch with me the other day on such short notice. I do hate to eat alone."

"Sure, Miranda. No problem," Jake replied. "It is a little odd for me to run into church folks during my hospital rounds. It's usually the sick ones I'm there for. What exactly brought you to that neck of the woods?" he asked.

"Visiting...a family member," Miranda replied vaguely.

Sure, Claire thought.

"Anyway, it was good to bump into you," Miranda said. "Maybe it'll happen again. That would be a pleasant coincidence, wouldn't it?"

"Mmmmm," Jake replied, distractedly. "Excuse me, Miranda." He dodged past her. Claire could see him looking around and hoped he was searching for her as she hurried to Gran's car with a satisfied smirk on her face. *Miranda had set the whole thing up. Jake hadn't known she was coming.*

Their eyes met just as she was stepping into the car.

"See you tomorrow," he mouthed over the sea of mingling people.

Claire nodded and gave a small wave. "Tomorrow," she mouthed back and gave him a quick thumbs-up.

Chapter Thirteen

The ceiling fan was spinning at its lowest setting, barely stirring the early morning air in Claire's small bedroom. If she really concentrated, she could pick out an individual blade and follow it all the way around its circular track several times before her eyes blurred and the blade blended in with the others.

She rolled over on her side and checked the clock on the nightstand, six a.m. She had been up for a couple of hours already. Daylight hadn't yet begun to creep into the room when she'd first awakened with a start from a nightmare. Jesse Nugent had been yelling and chasing her as she ran stumbling and tripping down the side of a mountain.

What if he didn't take the news well? Shooting the messenger wasn't unheard of, after all. She'd turned all this over and over in her head until the night-blackened room had begun to lighten to the bluish-gray of earliest dawn. Now the sun was well over the horizon and the day could begin. *Might as well get this over with.* Her feet hit the linoleum floor and she padded into the bathroom.

The hot shower relaxed a few muscles, but not her mind. When Claire appeared at the breakfast table, she was unusually quiet. Paw was getting a late start, she noticed. He sat thoughtfully, watching her pour milk into her cereal. Gran was in the garden, weeding in the cool of the morning before the sun rose too high. Paw nursed his cup of coffee, pouring the steaming liquid into his saucer before blowing it cool and gingerly returning it to the cup. He repeated the process several times as Claire crunched a crispy strip of bacon. Finally, he spoke.

"Gran tells me you're going to Mountain View today with the preacher and she said it's not exactly on church business."

Claire nodded. She'd been as vague as possible when Gran had questioned her as she got into bed the night before. Gran claimed she was only up to go to the bathroom, but Claire knew better. She didn't want to give away too much information about something that wasn't truly her business to tell. She could only guess what wild ideas Gran had concocted to fill in the huge gaps in Claire's explanation.

"Um-huh," Claire murmured as she swallowed the bacon and the lump in her throat.

Paw leaned back in the dining room chair and crossed one leg over the other at the knee. "Gran can't figure out what in the world y'all are up to." He grinned. "It's drivin' her crazy."

"I'll give her the details as soon as I think it's alright," Claire said. Paw nodded.

"Jesse Nugent lives in Mountain View."

Claire stopped chewing in mid-chomp.

Paw kept his eyes on his coffee and continued. "I gather there's something hush-hush goin' on. I reckon you're going up there has something to do with him and that his momma don't know about it yet, for whatever reason. I ain't got no idea what this is about, but you and Brother Jake just tread softly. There's fine people concerned. Whatever y'all are doin', good luck." He jammed his battered cap onto his head and left out the back door just as Jake Weston knocked on the front door.

Claire rushed to meet Jake on the porch and shuttled him away before Gran could make it around the house from the garden. "Should we take my car?" she asked.

"Nope. Ol' Brown will do just fine."

They rode without much talk for a while. They passed through Little Rock and the used-to-be small towns that bordered and ran into it. Claire looked out at a new subdivision with its rows of almost identical, stylish homes. It was all so clean and perfect. *And bland.*

"Look at that," Jake said, pointing out the passenger window. On top of a hill overlooking the newly finished houses was a weather-beaten, two story Colonial style farm house. Its black shingles were cracked and chipped, worn away by years of wind, hail, and sun. The front porch sagged in the middle like the back of an old horse, and the pillars that supported its roof were nearly bare of paint. *I'd love to have that house*, although for the life of her she didn't know why.

Jake's voice startled her as his words expressed her thoughts, "I've always wanted to buy an old falling down house and fix it up. There's just so much history and tradition in an old house. They don't make 'em like that anymore. That house is one of a kind, almost like it has a life of its own. It's seen so much. You know?"

And she did know. Jake had voiced her feelings exactly. She'd just never realized she had them before. Claire nodded, silently, waiting for Jake to continue. She could listen to him talk for hours and never grow tired of it.

"I always feel sad when I see an old house that's been let go. But at the same time, I'm glad it's there. Reminds us there was something here before us. That house was probably built when this was a dirt lane and it was the only building around. Everything's changed around it, but it's still here. This may sound weird, but I think it's comforting, in a way."

Claire watched him, his wrists resting easily atop the steering wheel. She could tell Jake was lost in thoughts of old houses and remodeling.

"Aren't there any houses like that in Dogwood? If you really wanted to, you could start working on one for yourself."

"The thing about Dogwood is people are still living in those old houses and the parsonage will do just fine for a bachelor like me. It's tiny, that's for sure. But how much room does one guy need?" Jake said, then added, "If I ever had a family, I'd try to find a bigger place, I guess."

"Let's see what's on the radio," Claire suggested hurriedly. She turned the large, old-fashioned silver radio knob. It gave a click and static-filled music crackled from the speakers.

"Bluegrass?" Claire said, her eyebrows rose in two skeptical arches.

"*Classic* bluegrass, mostly," Jake said, haughtily. "Although, once in a while, they do play some of the newer stuff on this station."

Claire laughed. "Isn't 'new bluegrass' an oxymoron or something?"

"Watch the name calling, Sister Burke!" Jake replied sternly. Claire laughed again, and stuffed her fingers in her ears to drown out the tune she was hearing.

"I don't think people are supposed to sound like that unless they just got kicked really hard in the shins or something. It's so whiny!"

"That's what we like to call *twang*," Jake answered. "Maybe it's an acquired taste but it'll grow on you since we've still got another three hours of driving." Claire let out a groan as they left another tiny community shrinking in the rearview mirror behind them.

For a long while there was nothing but flat, open farmland. A bright yellow crop duster buzzed across the cloudless sky like a giant bumblebee. Claire watched it whizzing towards them high overhead, then diving low to fertilize the rice field that ran alongside the highway. The plane covered the crops with a heavy mist, then shot back up into the air just long enough to cross the road. It came down again on the other side, skimming close to the ground. It did this each time it came to a road or a stand of trees that divided the rice fields from each other. Claire watched it bounce along until it finally disappeared from sight, landing somewhere in the distance. The fields went on for miles in every direction, vast and empty, except for the occasional tiny farmhouse springing up in the middle of the land, as if some farmer had dropped a wrong seed and a house had come up instead of the expected corn or rice or soybeans.

The smooth, green land around them began to give way to the gentle rise and fall of hills. The hills grew, pushing their way out of the ground more frequently as they became higher and higher, until they were no longer hills at all but mountains. The road that had cut a bold straight line across the farmers' fields was now forced to wind and weave its way along as best it could.

"It seems like it takes forever to get anywhere in the mountains," Claire said. Anything she could see ahead of them would disappear from sight several times as the highway curled itself around between steep rock walls and towering trees.

"Well, I'm not really in much of a hurry," Jake said languidly.

"Me either," Claire remarked. "I'm nervous about this whole thing."

"I'm not so much worried about what we'll find when we get there, really. I just meant I was enjoying the ride." Jake glanced at Claire and smiled. "You're easy to talk to. Sometimes people feel like they can't really say what they want in front of a preacher, so they don't say much of anything."

"I've been holding back a cussing fit all day, just for your sake," Claire said somberly. "But other than that, I guess I'd say you're pretty easy to be around, too."

"So, how'd your interview go?"

Claire was surprised Jake knew about her trip to Dallas. "Mrs. Millie told me," he explained.

Claire sighed. "Figures. Did she tell you to try and talk me out of taking the job? *If* they even offer it."

Jake shook his head. "She said she just wants you to do what will make you happiest." They came to a stop sign. Jake turned and looked directly into Claire's face. "I think she's worried about you. She said something about you seeming all out of sorts lately. Is the stress of hunting a job getting to you?" he asked.

There's a lot more getting to me than that. She tried to decide how to best phrase her answer so she wouldn't tell an outright lie. At least a half-truth was better than a straight-up untruth.

"Yeah, I guess that's it. I'm not sure I did very well with that interview." She told Jake how she'd somehow ended up telling a complete stranger a very personal story about her mother. He listened quietly until she finished with a sigh. "Who knows if I got the job or not? Guess we'll just have to see."

Jake drummed his long fingers on the steering wheel and frowned slightly. "What if Dallas doesn't work out? What will you try next?"

"Not a clue. I don't even want to think about that right now." Claire picked up the atlas that was lying in the seat between them. "We need to turn left at the next intersection, then it's ten more miles into Mountain View."

They began to pass little signs of the tourist industry that flourished in the small Ozark town. Rock shops selling crystals as big as basketballs dotted the highway, along with places that peddled everything from old glassware to rusted-over plowshares. *Junktique* was the term Claire saw on the signs. They passed another jumbled little flea market, topped a small hill, and coasted into downtown Mountain

View.

The town was set up like many older, small towns. The courthouse served as the hub of the city, anchoring the town square. Branching off from it were narrow streets crammed with shops and cafes, music stores and ice cream parlors. Claire thought how much fun it would be to wander down the sidewalks and peer in the shop windows with Jake, but quickly dismissed the fantasy.

They crept along slowly, people-watching as they went. No one hurried as they passed from storefront to storefront. Families with children lounged under the trees that circled the courthouse, eating funnel cakes. A crowd had gathered on the square. People hauled lawn chairs from their cars and positioned them on the grass under the shade trees.

"What's going on?" Claire asked.

"Roll down your window," Jake said. She turned the stiff handle and eased the reluctant window down. Strains of music floated in on the still afternoon air. Fiddle music. As Claire listened, guitars, mandolins, and dobros joined in.

She could barely see the musicians until they turned and drove alongside them. Through a gap in the crowd, Claire spotted a little cluster of men and women, some old and some young, playing bluegrass for their small, but appreciative, audience. Jake slowed the truck to a crawl as they crept by, soaking in the sound of "Will There Be Any Stars in My Crown?" played and sung with a distinctive Ozark accent.

"Dirty trick, I know," he said once they were beyond the sound of the song. "Mountain View does lots of bluegrass festivals. I figured you didn't know that. Sorry if I made your ears bleed or anything."

Claire turned from the window to face Jake. "You know, it's not really so bad. Maybe it's just better in person."

He smiled and replied, "It grows on you, just like a lot of things. You just think you don't like it because you're not *supposed* to like it."

She hummed a few bars of the song they'd heard, then said, "Are you ready to earn some stars for our crowns and find Mr. Jesse Nugent?"

"Poor theology, probably, but yeah, I guess we better get with it if we're going to get this all done and get back to Dogwood tonight. Get out that road map and start watching street signs. We're looking for Mountaintop Trail."

They wound their way to the outskirts of town, where houses were scattered about, perched on any flat space available. Dwellings became fewer and farther between the further they drove. The roads that turned off from the main highway to the left and right were getting smaller and most of them were unmarked. *What if we missed it?*

Just as Claire was about to broach this idea to Jake, he leaned forward, squinted and said, "What's that little sign off to the right say?"

Barely noticeable among the thick trees that lined the highway was a small, narrow lane. As they drew closer, Claire could make out the lettering on a rectangular sign nailed to a pine pole. Burnt into the block of wood were the words, "Mountaintop Trail" and underneath "Posted. No Trespassing."

"That's probably not a good sign," Claire mumbled. Jake turned down the lane, which was little more than a trail, which made her quite glad they had driven the truck and not her car.

On both sides of the truck, running as far as they could see down the lane before them, were dogwood trees. Spring had fully ripened into summer by now, none of the trees held onto even a single blossom. *Sad, I imagine it would be a beautiful sight to pass under a canopy of pink and white blooms.*

The incline steepened, and the old, brown truck strained as it made the climb. "Come on, Buddy," Jake coaxed. "It can't be much further." But the lane kept going, winding up and up until Claire wondered how anyone could live so far off the beaten path. Just then the trees opened up and the ground leveled off. There in a clearing, overlooking a panoramic view of the mountains, was the backside of a small log cabin.

Jake turned off the engine, "I think we should pray for wisdom."

Or speed, Claire couldn't help remembering her dream of the night before.

Jake bowed his head, Claire did the same. She waited for him to speak, then realized he was praying silently.

"OK, God, here goes, I'm not really sure yet why You wanted me to do this, but I think You did. So You're going to

have to help me. If You've got any special instructions, now would be a good time to tell me."

She sat in the quiet truck, hearing nothing but the sound of Jake's breathing and her own heartbeat thudding in her ears. One word came into her mind as clearly as if it had been spoken aloud. *Listen.*

Listen? What is that supposed to mean? Claire frowned. God should at least try to make sense once in a while.

Jake whispered an Amen. He took a deep breath and said, "You ready?"

At Claire's nod, they slid out of the truck and she met Jake on his side. She looked the cabin over as they crunched up the gravel driveway toward its back porch. The house was small and square, with a green tin roof. The cedar logs fit together neatly, and Claire guessed Jesse had built it himself.

"I think this is the back. I wonder why he'd want his driveway to lead to the back of his house?" Claire said, softly, noting an ancient gray Toyota pickup parked near the house.

They went around one side of the cabin and stepped into the front yard. "Ohhh," Claire breathed. An expansive view of the tree-lined Ozarks spread before them in the ripened green glory of summer. The cabin was perched only a few hundred feet from the edge of a sharp drop-off. Claire edged toward it curiously, as Jake headed toward the front porch that ran the length of the house.

Claire stepped to the edge of the precipice. She looked out at the sky. It seemed to be as much around her as above. It was an almost unbearably bright blue, with just a few wisps of clouds hanging here and there like snow white smoke. She wanted Jake to see this. "Jake, this view is just breath..."

She never saw what was coming.

"Unnhh!" Claire gasped as she hit the ground with a thud. The wind was knocked out of her and she found herself nose-to-wet-nose with the biggest dog she'd ever seen. It was shaggy, black, and the size of a Shetland pony. *Mauled to death on the side of a mountain*, passed through Claire's mind as she squeezed her eyes shut and braced for the attack.

But instead of teeth, Claire felt the warm, wet

sensation of the dog's slobbery tongue giving her a thorough licking. She would've almost preferred the teeth, especially considering the animal had a severe case of canine halitosis.

"Help!" she managed to squeak just before the dog licked her fervently on the lips.

"Get down, Otis, you big idiot. Get back here! NOW!!"

A sturdy looking man was topping the hill, slipping and sliding in his hurry. Claire caught a glimpse of him before the massive pink tongue swept across her face again. She recognized him from the pictures at Mrs. Lola Faye's. The sandy-blonde hair might be a bit farther back at the forehead and the creases around his eyes were deeper, but this was the man they were looking for.

Jesse was carrying a long, walking stick, and tapped the dog's giant head with it insistently. Otis, who was still giving Claire an enthusiastic spit bath, turned around with a look of surprise in his brown eyes. He dropped to his haunches, panting and smiling up at his master, quite proud of the hospitality he'd shown their visitor.

Jake had come running at the sound of Claire's cries. He helped Claire to her feet, as she vainly tried to dry the side of her head with her shirt sleeve. The dog must have been for a swim in a nearby creek leaving his belly wet and muddy, making Claire's predicament that much nastier.

"Are you OK?" Jake asked, obviously worried, but also attempting to suppress the amusement in his voice.

"OTIS! You jug-headed fool! I apologize, Miss. He's just a little excitable. He's not mean at all. Go to the house, Otis!" Jesse jabbed his walking stick toward the porch. Otis's huge head drooped and he whapped his massive tail on the grass apologetically before he lumbered away, dejected that his welcome wasn't appreciated.

"I'm OK, really. I get knocked down by animals more than the average person, I think," she said, recalling the day Jake had witnessed her encounter with Charlotte the calf. "What kind of dog is that, exactly?" Claire asked, wiping at a muddy paw print on her stomach.

"I don't really know. Found him on the side of the road down the mountain. My guess is he's gotta be part Great Dane to be that big. Why don't y'all have a seat on the porch and I'll get you a wet rag or something to try and clean up with."

He disappeared into the house, leaving Claire and Jake by themselves. There were two benches made from split pine logs on the opposite end of the porch from where Otis lay looking dolefully at them. Jake motioned towards one, and Claire backed carefully in that direction, keeping a watchful eye on Otis as she went.

It was then she first noticed all the animals. Wooden animals, thankfully. Lining the porch, leaning against the walls of the house, were bears, coyotes, raccoons, rabbits and other mountain-type animals, all carved from huge chunks of wood. Claire leaned over and touched the nearest one, a bear about four feet tall, created from a cedar log. The bark had been shaved away and someone had whittled, shaped, and molded a charming likeness of a brown bear from the heart of the tree. It even had glittering black beads for eyes.

Jesse reappeared, handed Claire a wash cloth and settled onto the bench next to them. He leaned back, crossed his ankles, and looked out at the treetops that were now glowing deep green in the afternoon light. "So, I guess you heard about me down in town."

Claire looked at Jake, who was obviously as confused as she.

"Get a lot of referrals from The Crow's Nest. Did you see the cougar? I just finished it last week. I've got another smaller one going in my shop in the house." He nodded towards a snarling wooden cougar prowling the far end of the porch and Claire realized the menagerie was for sale. He thought she and Jake were just another tourist couple in search of a novel souvenir to mark their trip to the Ozarks.

"It's amazing," Jake said, as he stood and started to meander through the carvings, touching and admiring them.

Claire was beginning to think he wasn't going to say anything about who they were or why they were here, when he suddenly shook the woodcarver's hand and said, "I'm Jake Weston, Sir. Brother Jake is what I'm called most of the time."

"Jesse Nugent," the other man replied with a searching look in his bright green eyes. Concern registered across his broad, friendly face. "Weston, I believe you're my momma's preacher. Is something wrong? Is she alright?"

"She's fine, Mr. Nugent."

"Jesse," he said, simply. "Jesse's fine, Preacher."

Jake took a deep breath. "Mind if we come in, Jesse?"

His blond brows rose in wonder and a hint of concern passed across his face. "Sure. Come on in."

Claire followed Jake and Jesse into a smallish living room that opened into an even smaller kitchen. The furniture was made of log frames and covered with thinning plaid cushions. The interior walls of the cabin were flat boards, left their natural reddish color. In fact, almost everything was wood toned, in both the interior and exterior of Jesse's home, including the floors and the ceilings. Just two photographs hung on the otherwise bare walls. One was of Mrs. Lola Faye. The other showed a small, tow-headed boy with vivid green eyes standing next to a tall, thickly built man with broad shoulders and a deeply tanned face. The little boy beamed and held a stringer of fish. The man was looking down at the boy, one hand resting on the child's shoulder. *Jesse and his father.*

Jesse lowered himself into a chair, still holding his walking stick and casting his eyes from Claire to Jake curiously. "What brings you and Mrs. Weston up Mountain View way?"

"Oh, I'm not Mrs. Weston," Claire interjected, flushing a deep scarlet. "I'm just a friend of Jake's...and your mother's."

"Did Momma send y'all up here? If something's wrong, just tell me."

Jake had been watching Claire closely, but now turned his attention to Jesse. The time had come to deliver their strange message. "Mrs. Lola Faye doesn't know we've come to see you today. Claire and I were asked to come find you on behalf of your wife."

Jesse's ruddy cheeks blanched. He leaned back in his chair, then forward again, and rested his head in his hands. Claire looked at Jake for some sign of what to do. Jake held up his hand. "Wait," he mouthed to her silently.

"You know Lori?" Jesse finally said, head still down, eyes on the floor. His voice was quiet, almost frightened, as if even saying her name were somehow dangerous.

"Yes, I've known her for several years. Ever since I moved to Dogwood," said Jake.

Jesse looked up quickly and met their eyes. There was a haunted look on his face as he asked, "How is she?"

Claire could see Jake composing himself, gathering his thoughts. She knew a quick flare gun prayer for guidance had just been shot toward Heaven, so she added another short plea for divine guidance to go along with Jake's. *Help us, Lord.*

"A lot of things have changed in Lori's life since you saw her last. Some good, some not."

Jake tentatively began relaying the information Deloris had given them. He unfolded the tale delicately, laying it out for Jesse carefully so each bit could be considered before the next was brought to light. The car wreck, the rehabilitation, Deloris's pregnancy, her move to Jesse's old home.

Finally, Jake told Jesse of Deloris's belief in God. The belief in repentance and redemption that had prompted her to send them.

"Lori wanted us to make the first contact, but she really wants to speak with you herself. She has no expectations, as far as I can tell, for what may come next. She just wants to tell you how sorry she is *and* for you to meet your son." Jake touched Claire's knee gently, and nodded toward Jesse, who still cradled his head in his hands.

"Mr. Nugent," Claire said, softly, "I know this is too much for one person to have to handle all at once. But, if you could just meet Joshua, you'd fall in love with him in a heartbeat. He knows your mom and they really like each other. I think finding out she is his grandmother would be a wonderful blessing," Claire said. "After the shock wore off, of course," she added, not knowing what else to say. "Deloris wants to tell her about everything, but she felt you needed to know first."

Jesse sat motionless for a long time, saying nothing, his eyes now fixed on the window behind Claire and Jake. When he finally spoke, he said very slowly, "I've wondered what Lori was doing, what became of her, thousands of times in the past eight years but I would've never imagined."

He stood and walked by them, stopping to look out the screen door. A rabbit poked its head out from behind a tree, then loped easily across the yard and disappeared into the brush on the other side.

"I have all these Posted signs and No Trespassing signs so the hunters won't come up here," he still clutched the walking stick, and began to tap it gently, rhythmically on the floor. It sounded like the soft ticking of a clock. "This is a safe place, up here on top of this mountain. So if the deer, rabbits and anything else can survive, and make it all the way to the top, they'll be left alone."

He kept his eyes on the treetops. The evening sun was starting to slip lower toward the horizon. Its orange light glowed in his eyes and lit his tense face in profile as he spoke.

"When I left Montana, I was just starting to climb out of the deepest ditch I'd ever been in. When I finally got out, I knew I had to make some changes so I'd never get that low again. Up here, it's quiet. Peaceful. I have time to think, and enough to do to keep from thinking too much." He tapped the walking stick against his temple. "I've got it all untangled."

Jesse stopped talking and turned toward Jake and Claire abruptly. "I need some time to think. Thank you for coming."

Jake took the hint and stood. Claire followed his lead, and they moved toward the door. Jesse held it open for them.

"Whatever you decide to do, we'll keep you in our prayers," Jake said, putting his hand on Jesse's strong shoulder as they passed.

Jesse nodded and followed them onto the porch. Otis stood and barked a deep, rumbling bark of excitement as Claire walked by. She hurried on, afraid to repeat their earlier encounter. Otis whined and lay back down sadly.

They left Jesse Nugent standing on his front porch, alone with his dog and his blessed solitude.

"I wonder what he'll do," Claire asked as they began their descent.

Jake sighed. "I have no idea."

"What *should* he do?" Claire ventured.

"Same answer as before," Jake said. He looked at Claire and smiled slightly. "Preachers don't have all the answers, either. You just have to listen more than you talk and hope God will fill in the gaps."

Listen. Must be the word of the day. Claire was about to ask Jake if he was getting hungry when her stomach growled loudly, doing the job for her.

Jake smiled and said, "Me, too. Wanna try that place we saw on the way in? I think Yancy's was the name."

"Sounds great," Claire replied.

They found the court square just as busy as when they'd gone through several hours before. A fiddle rollicked through a solo verse of "Big Rock Candy Mountain," as Jake eased into one of the few remaining parking spaces near Yancy's Soda Shoppe and Pharmacy.

When Claire opened the truck door, the heavy air, thick with humidity, covered her like a blanket.

"Ugh. It feels like a dog breathing on you," she said.

"I guess you'd know all about that, huh?" Jake joked. "Must be going to rain."

Jake pushed open one side of the double glass door and they stepped into the cool of Yancy's which boasted a sign saying it was the oldest soda shop/pharmacy in Arkansas, family owned and operated since 1916 according to the gold lettering.

Along the back wall were shelves of liquids, pills, creams, and ointments to suit any ailment. The pharmacist and his assistants were at work to their left, raised a step above the eating area. To one side, a roped-off area displayed medical treatments from days gone by. What seemed like hundreds of tiny bottles filled with different colored concoctions sparkled and winked at them, reflecting the late afternoon light that slanted in from the storefront window.

"I bet there's some genuine snake oil over there that will cure anything you've got," Jake said.

"I don't need snake oil. I've got Gran and her Dr. Tischner's mouthwash. She thinks it cures anything. Sore throats, colds, mouth ulcers. Rubs it on cuts, poison ivy...you name it. I think it's pretty much straight alcohol, really. She may even drink it; I'm not sure."

"Maybe you shouldn't tell such things to Mrs. Millie's pastor," Jake said with a wink as they settled onto the chrome counter stools in front of an old fashioned soda fountain.

"What can I get you two?" asked the mustachioed man behind the counter.

Jake scanned the menu that hung above them. Claire examined the large punched tin ceiling tiles while he made up his mind. They were silvery gray with stars, hearts, and other designs stamped on them.

"A double bacon-cheeseburger, fries, and a cherry

Coke," she heard Jake say.

"Same," she added when the man looked her way. He turned and rummaged around in a cooler under the counter, then pulled out two large, icy mugs. With a pull of the gleaming brass fountain handle, he filled them with soda, added a shot of cherry flavor, and topped them both with big, glossy red cherries.

"Here you go. I'll go get started on those burgers. Both doubles, right?"

Claire nodded, and Jake looked at her, obviously amused, as the man headed back to the kitchen.

"Not a salad kind of girl, huh?" he asked, grinning at her.

Claire looked straight into the honey colored eyes. "Well, maybe if I were trying to make you think I was a delicate, dainty flower of a girl but I'm pretty sure it's too late for that." She pointed to the still visible mud stains on her shirt and jeans. "You can work up quite an appetite getting wrestled by a Great Dane. I think I'll find the restroom and try to clean up a little bit."

Claire returned from her vain attempt at tidying up still struggling with her tangled hair. She sat down beside Jake, pulled the ponytail holder out and tried to smooth the mass of red waves. Jake watched appreciatively.

"My hair even smells like dog!" Claire griped. Jake leaned over, lifted an auburn curl and sniffed thoughtfully.

"Honeysuckle and roses."

"Yeah, right," Claire replied, flustered. Jake held the lock of hair and rolled it between his fingers for a few more seconds.

Their server reappeared, carrying two burgers roughly the size of hubcaps.

They did their best, but still left half of the food behind with their tip when they staggered out half an hour later, entirely too full, but happy about it.

"It's good to be headed back south," Jake said as Mountain View grew smaller and smaller in the rearview mirror. They didn't say much for a while.

Jesse, Deloris, and Joshua were on her minds, so she was glad they rode together in silence. Claire couldn't help but think Jake was one of the few people she could be around and not feel compelled to make small talk with. She looked out into the fading daylight and read the passing road signs

Now leaving Mountain View, Ya'll Come Again!

Waverly-15 Miles

Elk Preserve-1 Mile.

"Did that say 'Elk Preserve?'"

"What?" Jake asked, brought from deep reverie by Claire's question. "Where?"

"That road sign. It had the outline of an elk and I think it said, 'Elk Preserve, one mile.' What in the world does that mean?"

Jake thought for a minute. "Oh, I know. The Game and Fish Commission has a little elk herd up in this part of the state. They used to be native to the state before hunters wiped them out. You can look at them and take pictures and things, if I remember right. We can stop and have a look, if you want. That is if you're not in too big a hurry to get home." The hopeful note in his voice was evident.

"Here's comes another sign. It says they're going to be on our right. Oh! There they are!"

A spacious pasture spread before them. In the dusky purple light, a small herd of elk were feeding behind a wooden fence. Jake turned his headlights on so they could get a better look. There was a little gazebo for elk watchers to sit under, but Claire was already scrambling to the top of the fence. She perched carefully on the top rail and called for Jake to join her. He slung his long legs over the fence with ease and sat beside her.

"They're beautiful," she'd never realized how huge a bull elk was until she watched the largest of the herd meander by. His antlers were massive, wide, thick, and tall. A childlike thought passed through Claire's mind. The antlers looked like a throne where you could sit and ride around like a queen. She admired the deep chocolate shade of the bull elk's face, noticing how it faded to a light tawny brown along his middle. A female sidled up to the bull and began feeding beside him. The darkness deepened around them, but neither the animals nor the people who sat quietly observing them noticed.

"Wish I had my camera," Jake said at last. "Don't see many elk in Arkansas."

"But they look right at home, don't they?" Claire

commented, watching a young calf and its mother settling into a patch of wild heather. "I think it's too dark for pictures now."

They both looked around and realized that night had stolen in and relieved the evening of its post without their notice.

"We better get going. Gran will be chomping at the bit to grill me on what we've been up to." Jake agreed and said he wanted to see Deloris before he turned in for the night, just to let her know how things went.

"Honestly, I'm not sure what to say, 'cause I don't know how it went and I was there," he said as they slammed the doors of Ol' Brown.

Jake turned the key.

Nothing.

He tried again, expecting to hear the loud grumbling of the old motor as it roused itself from rest. Nothing happened. Frowning, he gave the key a few more futile turns, then slumped back against the seat. Claire peered at him, trying to see the expression on his face in the dark cab.

"Battery's dead," he said, bluntly, a hint of annoyance edging his voice. "I shouldn't have left the lights on so long. Must've sat there watching the elk longer than I thought."

Claire mimicked his defeated posture as she wondered what to do next. "Oh, I know! I'll use my cell phone and call information. They can give us the name of a service station or something." She dug around in her purse and triumphantly retrieved her phone.

The screen read "No Service".

Jake looked completely unsurprised by this development. "We're surrounded by trees and mountain peaks, plus where we are now is kinda in a hollow. You'd need to know Morse code to get a message out of here. We'll just have to wait until someone comes by and try to flag them down for a jump."

Claire didn't say it, but in the entire time they'd been at the Elk Preserve, not a single car had passed. Jake sighed wearily, shoved the truck door open, and jumped out. Not knowing what else to do, Claire followed.

She found him sitting on the lowered tail gate. The frustration was gone from his face, and now he appeared to be lost in contemplation. Claire hopped up beside him. "Now what?" she asked.

"I think there's an old quilt behind the seat. I used it at a church hayride last fall. Pretty sure I never got it out."

He scrambled down from the tail gate and soon returned with the tattered quilt, folded over several times to make a soft seat for them.

They settled down on the quilt, side by side. Claire glanced up at the sky. Thick clouds had rolled in after sunset, smothering the stars and hiding many of them from view. The clouds were trying their best to wrestle the moon down for the night, too, and when they succeeded, it would be dark as a cave. The moon wasn't ready to turn in just yet. It reappeared over and over again, casting a pale yellow glow over the two travelers, who were now lying on their backs, watching it in silence. The moose had lowered themselves into their grass beds for the night, rear ends settling down first, then bending the front legs and completing the process, like larger versions of Paw's cows.

"You know," Jake said at last, "I guess there are worse people to be stranded in the mountains with."

"Thanks. I think," Claire replied. She knew what he meant. "But it's not gonna look very good if some parishioner sees us sneaking into town in the wee morning hours, huh?"

"Nope."

Claire watched the moon elude the clouds again. "Do you ever wish you weren't a preacher?"

Jake thought for a while. In the moonlight, she could see a slight smile skip across his face before he answered. "Maybe sometimes. But then I think that would be like wishing I wasn't myself. It's just who I'm supposed to be."

A low rumble in the distance made Claire sit straight up. "Was that a car?"

The sound grew deeper and more forceful, then stopped.

"Thunder," Jake said.

A second later, the bottom fell out. They had been ambushed by a sneak attack from a summer thunderstorm.

"Get under that gazebo," Jake said as he snatched up their blanket and dashed for cover with Claire at his heels.

Dripping and sputtering, Claire plopped down on the gazebo's picnic table. The rain beat down like countless hammers, pounding against the green tin roof. Speaking in less than a shout was pointless. They sat on the picnic table in the center of the gazebo and waited.

Within ten minutes, the torrent had eased into a steady, soft rhythm. The moon had given up completely now and it was totally dark around them. Claire fished in her pocket for her cell phone. She couldn't believe it had remained dry. She shone its tiny flashlight toward Jake.

"The batteries won't last long on this. I just wanted to see if you were drowned over there."

"Not quite. What was it Mr. Burke said the other day at dinner? Rain on the first, rain fifteen more days in the month? I guess we were due."

"I better turn this off or I won't have any batteries left to call home in the morning." The phone chimed as she shut the power off. They sat in the blackness and listened to the rain, now softening to a patter.

"It's not so bad, really. I kind of like the rain," Claire said. "But I wouldn't want to be here alone."

"Nope."

Jake told her about being alone in a canoe on the river in a downpour. "I couldn't decide whether to bail or paddle. I made it to the bank, but that's the last time I've been out by myself like that."

They spent the next several hours talking about everything, and nothing. Jake did most of the talking, and Claire, for once, was the listener.

"I have a confession to make," Jake said at last.

"Don't tell me you stranded us on purpose," Claire kidded.

"No, I'm not that clever," he replied. "But I wish I were. I've actually enjoyed tonight a whole lot. It was just what the doctor ordered. Well, the Great Physician, more likely."

"How's that?" Claire asked, intrigued.

"It's not easy to be Brother Weston every minute of the day. Tonight, I got to be Jake. Just plain old Jake."

Claire didn't know how to respond to this. She was touched, a little embarrassed, and grateful it was dark so he couldn't see that blasted blush creeping up her cheeks. She elbowed him in the ribs gently and said, "Glad to be of service."

It was either very late or very early when a peaceful lull fell over their conversation. The once boiling rain had now simmered down to a gentle sprinkle.

Both bleary eyed and tired, they sat side by side with the quilt over their knees in the chill left after the rain. Jake began to hum softly.

"What's that song?" Claire asked, yawning.

"*Simple Gifts*. The fiddlers were playing it when we left Yancy's."

Claire listened to the deep, calming notes. "It sounds familiar."

"You've probably heard it around Thanksgiving. I thought it was kind of interesting to hear an old Shaker hymn played on a fiddle in the Ozarks."

She laughed. "You a big fan of old Shaker hymns or something?"

"Hymnody. Took it as an elective in seminary."

"Would you mind singing it for me? I don't think I've ever heard the words."

Jake hesitated. "Only for you. Remember, I took Hymnody, not Vocal Performance. One verse is all I'm doing." He cleared his throat and began singing slowly, shyly, in a soft baritone.

'*Tis the gift to be simple*
'*Tis the gift to be free*
'*Tis the gift to come down where you ought to be*
And when we find ourselves in the place just right
It will be in the valley of love and delight
When true simplicity is gained
To bow and to bend we shan't be ashamed
To turn, turn will be our delight
'*Til by turning, turning we come round right.*

****

When the final note died away, there was a deep, still quiet. The moon made a brief reappearance as Jake leaned toward Claire and tried to make out her features in the faint light. He was distressed to see a single tear slip down her cheek.

"Was it that bad?"

"No, no at all," she said.

"Then what's the matter?"

She heaved a deep sigh. "I don't know where I ought to be. I thought I did, but now I'm not sure. It's like my 'place just right' relocated and didn't bother to tell me."

Jake reached out and took her hand in his. When she

didn't pull away, he gave it a gentle squeeze.

"Maybe it's right where it has been all along. Don't make things harder than they are, Claire. If you know where you're happy and what brings you joy, that's a gift. Even if it doesn't go with the original plan you had."

Claire sniffed, then laid her head on his shoulder. So much was still undecided, up in the air. She hated the feeling of not being in control. But at this moment, none of it mattered too much, somehow. Her weary burning eyes closed, as she fell asleep.

Jake felt her relax against him. He carefully pulled the quilt over her shoulder, and looked at their hands, still joined together. Brother Jake Weston smiled, gave Claire's hand a little squeeze, and prayed a prayer of thanksgiving.

Chapter Fourteen

Claire awoke an hour later to the sound of a car engine purring nearby. Her neck was stiff and she was more than a little embarrassed to realize she'd been snuggled up on Jake's shoulder sound asleep. She jumped up from the picnic table and almost crashed into the bench beside it, unaware her leg had fallen asleep. Staggering and stammering, she finally steadied herself and said, "Guess I must've nodded off. I bet you did too, huh?"

"Nope."

Claire went through the usually calming ritual of tightening her ponytail and found it didn't help much this time. "Where'd that car come from?"

A gray Buick with Louisiana plates was parked next to Jake's truck. A middle-aged man was rummaging through the trunk. He emerged holding his jumper cables in triumph. "Found 'em."

"These nice folks happened by. They're driving all night to get to Branson. They pulled over to check their map, saw the truck, and came over to see if we needed help."

Claire realized she'd slept on Jake's shoulder through all this. "Why didn't you wake me up?" she demanded.

"Just letting you get some rest. Sleep is spiritual, you know. Don't try to make any big decisions in life when you're give out."

Their conversation just before she'd fallen asleep replayed in her mind. "I won't," she promised.

A few minutes later, the brown truck roared to life. "Thank you so much!" Claire exclaimed. She checked her watch in the headlight's glow. Two in the morning.

"We really appreciate this. Hope y'all have a good trip."

"Y'all, too!" said the tourists as Claire once again clambered into the truck and they headed south considerably faster than they'd traveled the day before.

Claire tried holding her phone just right, but still

couldn't get enough of a signal to call home. She hated to call at this hour, but she knew Gran and Paw would be worried sick. It was almost three o'clock when she finally managed to make a fuzzy connection with Gran.

"Gran! Gran! Can you hear me?" Claire shouted.

"Good Lord, Claire Elizabeth! Where have you been? I would've done called the law if you weren't with the preacher. Are y'all okay? What happened to you? Where've you been?"

Claire deciphered most of what Gran was yelling through the fuzz and breaks on the line and was able to make her understand the basics of her and Jake's adventure.

"ELK? Did you say elk?" Gran hollered back. "Oh, never mind. Just get home quick as you can.

****

Claire awoke with the midday sun streaming in through the eyelet curtains. She squinted at the clock. Almost noon.

She sat up, rubbing her eyes. Gran's head peeped around the edge of the bedroom door. "You up?" she asked, softly.

"Barely," Claire answered with a yawn. "I'm not made for late nights."

Gran offered no comment, which got Claire's full attention. Her grandmother was watching the breeze lift the curtains over Claire's bed.

"You're awfully quiet," Claire ventured.

"That Mr. Johnson from the hospital called this morning. Said he'd like to speak with you today, if it's convenient. Said he had good news."

It was Claire's turn at playing the quiet game, it seemed. She found herself totally bereft of words.

"Did you hear me, Claire? Claire?"

"I heard you, Gran."

Neither spoke for a little while. "I think I'm ready for some breakfast. Or dinner," Claire said at last. She wrapped a robe around her faded pajamas and headed for the kitchen.

Her preemptive strike against unwanted advice worked. Gran held her peace, and Claire was starting to think she'd be able to enjoy a leisurely pork chop dinner when a familiar rumble drifted through the screen door.

126

Claire hurried to the front porch, running her hand through her hair as she went. It turned out that pork grease didn't make the best styling product, but she was too distracted to notice.

Jake was coming up the sidewalk, his long strides a bit slower than usual. The late night showed on his face, but he looked content and happy nonetheless.

"Good afternoon, Mrs. Burke," he said to Gran, who had followed Claire onto the porch. "Mind if I borrow Claire for a while?"

"Are you gonna haul her off to look at moose or some such and keep her out until the wee hours?"

"Don't plan on it," Jake said with a grin and a subtle wink at Claire, who skittered back into her room and dressed at warp speed.

Claire jumped into the truck with a practiced leap. She was getting good at this. She knew without asking that they were going to see Deloris. They discussed their visit with Jesse at length as they drove. When a loaded log truck passed them, Claire realized they were driving painfully slow. Jake was in no hurry to recount their meeting with Jesse to his estranged wife.

"What're you going to tell her?" Claire asked.

"Not sure yet," Jake replied. "I think all I can say is we delivered her message, Jesse heard us out. Whether he'll come and meet with her face to face, I just can't say."

"I can," Claire said, pointing towards the little white house as it came into view. Parked in front was an old, gray Toyota pickup. Otis lay spread across the length of the tailgate, napping in the sunshine.

Jake slowed the truck to a stop, put it in reverse, and backed up the long driveway.

"He must've left pretty soon after we did," Jake noted. Claire wondered what was being said by Deloris and Jesse. It seemed too delicate a subject to speculate on, so Claire kept her wonderings to herself and said a little prayer that nothing rash would be said or done.

Jake hummed a few bars of "Simple Gifts" as they bounced along. Claire's mind was on her upcoming phone conversation with Jasper Johnson. What would she say to him? From the way Gran talked, it sounded like he'd phoned to tell her she had the job, if she wanted it. *Do I want it?*

Absently, she reached up and pulled down the sun visor. A faded Jessamine blossom fell into her lap. The once vibrant color had softened to a pale yellow. The scent, though not nearly as intense, still lingered.

She cupped the bloom delicately in her hand. Glancing at Jake, who hadn't seen the flower fall, she said, "Look what I just found."

When he saw what she was holding, he colored slightly. Seeing Jake do the blushing for once was encouraging. "Why did you take me to the creek that day?" she blurted.

He didn't answer for a long minute. "Because I just knew you would love it there."

Claire turned the delicate petals over in her hands. "How did you know?"

Jake briefly met her questioning eyes with his honest, direct gaze, before turning his attention back to driving.

"Some things, you just...*know.* You know?"

"Yeah," she replied. She looked out the window and watched the passing fields. The land was beginning to flatten out now. Hayfields and pines with an occasional cow pasture came into view. She had a sudden surge of emotion, as if she were coming home from a long journey.

"Yeah, I think I do know."

When Claire stepped into the living room, she prepared herself for the cross examination. After this much time, there was no way Gran would let the Mountain View excursion pass without a few well-aimed questions.

Gran proved her wrong. She seemed preoccupied and didn't ask a thing about her granddaughter's mysterious doings. Her only comment on the whole ordeal came as she carried a basket of laundry out the backdoor to the clothesline.

"Girl, I have no idea what you got yourself into last night. Your clothes looked like something the dog drug under the porch and wallered."

Later, when Claire awoke from a short power nap, she found Gran standing at the kitchen sink, running the flat edge of a knife over the taut red skin of a tomato. Claire watched as she deftly flipped the knife over and peeled the now loose skin with a few, short strokes. She plopped the squishy ball into a colander, where it waited with the rest of the crop to be cooked, cooled, mashed, and canned. Claire watched her, head bent over her work, peeling the tomatoes more and more slowly.

"Gran, are you okay?" Claire asked.

"I'm fine, sugar. I'm just a little dizzy. Must've stayed in the sun too long when I was out in the garden."

She stopped and leaned heavily against the sink. Wiping her dripping hands, Gran turned and went towards the living room. Claire followed. "I think I'll just close my eyes for a while. I'll finish them tomatoes later," she said as she sank into Paw's recliner.

"Where's Paw?" Claire asked.

"Out in the barn. He's movin' that bottle calf out with the herd today."

Claire started out the door. She thought Paw should know Gran wasn't feeling well so he could drop in and check on her.

"You better call that man back about the job. It don't look good to not return a call that important as soon as you can."

"Okay, Gran, I will." Claire picked up her cell phone from the coffee table, took the paper with Jasper Johnson's number from the desk where Gran had written it and started toward the barn.

She found Paw's trailer backed up to the barn door. Paw was expertly herding Charlotte toward the open gate of the trailer. When the little heifer saw Claire, she bolted.

"Dang fool!" Paw had her down with one swift grab at the heels. He armed up the bawling, white calf as if she weighed twenty pounds instead of one hundred and twenty. He dumped Charlotte rather unceremoniously into the trailer and shut the door with a clank.

"Finally decided to get up today, I see" he said, wiping the sweat from his eyes with his sleeve.

"Even Sleeping Beauty has to wake up eventually" she joked. "I thought I better come find you. Gran said she was dizzy. Maybe you could stop by and check on her in a little while."

Paw nodded. "I'll see about her after while. I'm goin' to doctor a sick one and unload this calf. I'd say you could come, but she's mighty spooky. Acts awful nervous around you."

Claire walked to the trailer and stuck her hand between

the bars. "You're not scared of me, are you Charlotte?"

Meeeerrrr! Charlotte pranced to the opposite end of the trailer and lay down with her back to Claire. Claire followed her and was able to scratch the calf's head before Charlotte maneuvered just out of her reach.

Paw shook his head. "Hard-headed little joker."

"Oh, she's a sweet calf and she's not scared of me. We just had an unfortunate encounter, that's all."

"Who said I was talking about the calf?" Paw said, laughing to himself as he rattled away.

Claire put her hands on her hips indignantly. "You just bought yourself unsweetened tea for supper with that comment, Buddy!" she hollered after him.

She climbed over the fence next to the barn and set off across the pasture, following one of the cow trails. The narrow grassless paths made by hundreds of hooves treading the same path day after day, year after year, criss-crossed the field. A haze of light brown dust rose around her feet as she walked, her hands in her blue jeans' pockets.

Soon she was standing at the top of the hill that rose gently skyward in the center of the pasture. The trail she'd been following broke into several divergent paths that ran down the hill this way and that, snaking and winding to the bottom where the cows were now gazing contentedly in the afternoon sun. A soft breeze rippled through the grass and stirred the tendrils that played around her face.

Claire settled herself in a patch of thick green grass. Intertwined with the grass were multitudes of small flowers, bright citrine in color and as shiny as if they had been lacquered. *What are they called?* She couldn't think right now what Paw had said their name was.

Opening her flip phone, she dug Jasper Johnson's number out of her pocket and dialed.

The call was short and to the point. Mr. Johnson was prepared to offer Claire the job and he set forth the attractive terms and benefits succinctly. It was quite an opportunity for a young person just out of school with great potential for advancement, and he had graciously allowed her time to think before making her decision.

Claire picked a flower and spun it between her thumb and forefinger. It was the exact color of the jasmine. Bitterweed. That's what they were called. *What made them weeds and not flowers?* She looked up and saw patches of gold scattered across the entire pasture. It looked like sunshine had been seeded on the ground, taken root and spread.

"Yes, I'd like a day to consider. I'll let you know tomorrow."

She hung up, lay back, and closed her eyes. The warm sun shone across her face and she closed her eyes even tighter against its brightness. *OK, God. I'm listening. That's what I'm supposed to do, right? Feel free to say something.*

Nothing. The previous day's adventures in Mountain View whirled through her head. She thought of Mrs. Lola Faye, of the changes that were likely to come her way in the next few days. *What was it Mrs. Lola Faye had said about knowing what to do?* Sometimes, you just don't know until you do it. Claire didn't think she liked that advice very much. The first sermon she'd heard Jake preach wafted through her mind.

Maybe God didn't really care where she went to work. It came to her rather suddenly that she'd been so wrapped up in her Dallas dilemma that she'd not said much to God lately aside from pestering Him to tell her what to do in this area. She began to pray again, but this time words of gratitude formed in her mind.

Thank you, Father, for my family. For Gran and Paw. For the love and stability they've given me all my life. Thank You for this farm. For Dogwood Church. Thank You for Mrs. Lola Faye coming into my life, and allowing me to come into hers. And for letting me meet Jake.

She thought about all the people and places that were most precious to her, and the man who was growing more and more so every day, and felt an overwhelming sense of gratitude and joy. They were all right here, bundled together in this little community. All right here at home. This felt like home, and it always had.

Claire relaxed and felt herself sink deeper into the grass. She knew what she would do. She would talk to Paw about selling her an acre or two of his land. She could build herself a little house and commute to work. Driving to Little Rock every day wasn't so bad if that's what she had to do. She breathed a relieved sigh. It would all work out.

This hilltop would be a perfect house place, she thought,

happy to have made up her mind at last.

Jumping to her feet, she started toward the house. Her dad would be disappointed, no doubt about it. She didn't look forward to telling him. But Gran and Paw would understand.

Claire decided to talk to Paw about the house idea at once. *No, I want to tell Jake first. I think he'll be excited to hear I'm staying around. At least, I hope he will.*

It was almost more than she could allow herself to hope for, but the faint excited fluttering in her stomach refused to go away. Maybe it wasn't too late for them. She would understand if he wanted nothing to do with her, but just maybe.

Taking a deep breath, she increased her pace and, since no one was looking, even skipped a few feet before she came within sight of the house. Paw's four wheeler was parked under the shade tree in the yard. He must have come to check on Gran. *Good. Maybe he'll still be in when I get back.* She slid into the steamy interior of her car, rolled down the windows, and started toward Dogwood Church.

The nervous energy and excitement that raced through Claire's body made her almost giddy as she sped along the highway. She couldn't stop beaming, and happily tried to anticipate Jake's reaction to her big news. Thinking of his wide smile and warm hazel eyes made it difficult to pay attention to anything else. Even the shiny red Mustang convertible, only partially hidden by the church van in the parking lot, escaped Claire's notice.

Jake would be in his office, making notes and reading up for his next sermon. She felt certain of finding him there.

The window that looked out from the pastor's office onto the church yard was covered with Venetian blinds, opened to let in the June sunlight. Claire hurried up the sidewalk, almost running. Suddenly, she came to a dead stop.

Through the blinds, she saw two figures. Jake was standing, facing the window, deep in conversation with someone. There was no mistaking the perfect figure of Miranda Davenport. Claire's already pounding heart kicked into double-time staccato rhythm.

Jake was looking intently at Miranda. He nodded a few times, his head turned slightly to the side, as was his habit when he was really listening. A small smile curved his lips.

What could she be saying to him? Miranda's back was turned toward the window.

Claire's mouth went dry as she saw Miranda's hand come to rest on Jake's shoulder. The shoulder she'd slept on just one night past. Surely he'd brush her hand off and step away. *Why isn't he walking away?* Miranda took a half step closer. They were dangerously near each other. Jake was looking down into Miranda's eyes. She tilted her beautiful face upward...

A hot, sick sensation burned through her body as Claire realized what was about to happen. She turned and fled down the sidewalk before the inevitable kiss could take place. Her eyes filled with searing tears as she flung herself into her car and sped away.

A sob shook her shoulders as she drove furiously towards home. Wretched feelings of pain, anger, and embarrassment took turns providing fuel for her tears. This couldn't be happening. *How could he have fallen for someone so phony, so disgustingly, obviously, fake and conniving?* In her brief dealings with Miranda Davenport, she had seen more than enough to have her number. *Why hadn't Jake?*

It was because she was so beautiful, Claire thought, bitterly. A glance in the rearview mirror showed puffy red eyes and a face blotchy from crying. No wonder Jake was drawn to Miranda. She was certainly no competition for such beauty, however artificial it might be. *But why had Jake made his gentle advances if he'd really wanted Miranda?* Thoughts of the creek bank sprung unbidden to her mind, bringing a fresh shower of tears.

She slammed her car into park in front of Paw and Gran's house and rushed under the trees where the mockingbirds greeted her with their mingled songs. She kept her eyes to the ground and hurried on, flinging open the screen door with a crash.

She wouldn't let anyone see her like this. She'd go to her room until she got it together. Gran was probably still in the kitchen. Claire wanted to avoid her and Paw if she could.

But Gran was nowhere to be found. Neither was Paw. The house was oddly still. She hurried through the living room and into the kitchen. Where was everyone? Something crushed under her foot. Paw's cap, sweat-stained and covered with dirt. *What is it doing in the middle of the floor?*

A jolt of fear shot through her stomach. Instinctively, she knew something was wrong.

In the next second, she heard Paw speaking somewhere in the back of the house, his words strained with fear. Claire ran toward the sound of Paw's terrified voice. "Hold on, Millie. They'll be here in a minute. Hold on, Millie."

She found Gran lying on the bedroom floor, drenched in sweat, groaning in pain. Her wet house dress stuck to her body, her apron spread around her on the floor like a fallen leaf. A gash on her head glared angry red against her pallid skin, evidence of a fall against the corner of the dresser. Claire knelt beside Gran, next to Paw.

"What happened?" she asked, noting Gran's almost corpselike color.

Paw ran a shaking hand across his face. "I come in to check on her and I heard her holler out, like she was hurt. Then I heard her fall, I found her just like this. I called the ambulance already."

"Gran," Claire said in a calm voice. Her training took over, steadying her, allowing her to assess Gran's condition calmly. "Where do you hurt?"

Gran opened her eyes. The grimace of pain on her face tightened as she tried to speak. "Between my shoulder blades. I come back here to lie down. So dizzy, and...started hurtin'...real bad. Then I fell."

"It's alright. Don't talk. I'll be right back." Claire hurried into the bathroom and rifled through the medicine cabinet. She found what she was looking for and returned.

"Gran, I think you may be having a heart attack. I've got four aspirin here. I need you to chew them up and swallow them. They'll thin the blood while we wait for the paramedics."

Carefully, Claire placed her grandmother's head on her lap and gave her the aspirin. Gran chewed them dutifully, and swallowed as best she could.

"It's best to take them without water, if you can," Claire said, stroking Gran's damp hair. Gran nodded, and closed her eyes again. Her lips were a thin white line, her face still deathly pale. Claire had to turn her eyes. She looked at Paw, who was standing in the doorway of the bedroom, clenching and unclenching his hands in frustration. His Millie was hurting, and there was nothing he could do to help her.

"I hear them. I hear the sirens!" he cried, rushing to the front door and out into the yard. He picked his cap up on the way used it to hail the ambulance before showing the paramedics into the room with their equipment.

"I'm a nurse. I think she's having an MCI. Symptoms are profuse sweating, intense pain between the shoulder blades, and dizziness. She's had four aspirin." Claire answered the paramedics' question with steadiness and authority as they maneuvered around the tiny bedroom and loaded Gran onto a stretcher. The hurried voices of the paramedics, the shuffling of instruments and bags, and the metallic rattle of the clattering stretcher filled the house.

Paw climbed into the back of the ambulance. Claire watched him squeeze Gran's hand before the doors were shut and they were lost from her sight.

She stood on the porch, listening to the wail of the siren as it faded into the distance. Without thinking, she started toward her car. She had to get to the hospital. Gran needed her. Paw needed her. Someone would have to tell her dad. She began the longest drive of her life to St. Bernadette Memorial Hospital, praying all the way with an earnestness and intensity she didn't know she possessed.

Chapter Fifteen

They sat together in a corner of the waiting room, staring at the floor. A TV blared on and on, tuned to a sports station, giving the vital statistics of another all-important basketball game. Paw and Monroe were seated side by side, waiting for a report from Gran's surgeon.

Paw was quiet, as usual. His son was uncharacteristically so. Two pairs of broad hands, one calloused, one smooth, busied themselves with useless motion. Paw twisted his grimy cap; Monroe did the same with his silk tie.

Claire paced, watching them. She was glad her father had been in a meeting close by when she'd reached him on his cell phone. He had arrived at the hospital even before she did. His usual brashness was gone, quieted by concern and love for his momma. He looked, Claire thought, vulnerable. She'd seen this look only once before, when her mother was nearing the end.

She eased gently into the chair beside him. Silently, she took his hand and gave it a little squeeze. He patted her knee. "I'm so glad you were there, Claire. You knew what to do. The paramedics told Daddy your giving her the aspirin probably saved her life." He gave her a gentle smile. "Your mother was right. You'll make a fine nurse."

"Burke family?" The doctor was coming toward them. "I'm Dr. Robbins."

Monroe and Paw stood at the same time.

"Is she gonna be alright?" Paw closed his eyes as if waiting for a blow to land and waited for the answer.

"Your wife had a myocardial infarction, a heart attack. There was a seventy percent blockage. We inserted stents and she came through the surgery well. Now, there is some damage to the heart muscle. But things could've been much worse. As it stands, the prognosis is good for a full recovery."

"Thank you. Thank you so much, Doctor," Monroe said,

shaking the doctor's hand with the unabashed enthusiasm of a used-car salesman.

Claire couldn't help smiling to herself. Crisis seemed to bring out a better side of her father. Maybe it just brought out the real side.

She looked at Paw. He let out the breath he'd been holding since Dr. Robbins started speaking and sank back into his chair. His hands were still now, clasped in silent prayer, as he gave his thanks to another, greater Healer.

When they were allowed to see Gran several hours later, she was newly settled in her own room. They found her groggy from surgery, but alert enough to talk.

"How're you feeling, Gran?" Claire asked, holding her hand carefully, avoiding the IV stuck into one of the deep purple veins that showed under Gran's thin skin.

"My mouth's so dry I can't tell you," Gran said. Claire handed her a glass of water. A small sip and she was ready to talk, although more slowly and quietly than usual. "Had a heart attack, I hear."

Claire nodded. Gran looked at Paw and Monroe for a few quiet seconds.

"But I'm gonna make it?" It was more of a question than a statement. The men nodded.

"The doctor had a very encouraging report. Your chances of recovery are excellent," Monroe said as he settled into a chair next to her bed.

Gran mulled this over. "They're gonna try to make me eat tofu and all that food that ain't even food, I reckon." She sighed deeply. "Well, I can try. But I ain't makin' any promises. There's only so much a person can tolerate."

"I don't think you'll be limited to bean sprouts and water, Gran," Claire said with a small laugh. She was glad to see Gran was going to be her old self again soon, if not in body then certainly in attitude. "But a few changes won't hurt."

Gran cast a despairing glance at Paw, seeking support against the attack on their bacon grease and butter. He was still too shaken from the ordeal to think of anything besides what had just happened, and what could've happened.

"You look like you've lost your best friend, Franklin," Gran said.

Paw reached down and took the thin, white hand in his

burly, tanned one. Gran placed it to her lips. "And you might've come pretty close. But I'm still here for now, so don't be takin' out no personal ads just yet."

"Mother, none of us think this is a joking matter," Monroe said sternly. Gran turned to look at him.

The faintest flicker of a smile played at the corner of Gran's lips as she said, "Who said I was joking? Your daddy couldn't live without me. He'd starve out in three days, tops. He'd have to find him another woman pretty quick or he'd never have any food. Or clean clothes. Or clean dishes. And nobody to can all the garden stuff." Her voice trailed off.

"You're getting tired. Why don't we just step out and let you get some rest?" Claire suggested.

Gran closed her eyes. "Do whatever you want but I'm not gonna run you off. If I can sleep through your Paw's snoring, I can sleep through y'all visiting." In less than a minute, she was snoring.

Claire and Monroe rose to leave. Paw stayed where he was, standing over Gran's bed, watching the rise and fall of her chest. "You two go on. Get you somethin' to eat. I'm gonna stay with her."

Down in the hospital cafeteria, Monroe and Claire settled into a booth and picked at their food. Monroe spoke first. "Heard you had a job offer in Dallas."

Claire lifted her eyes to meet his gaze. *If he starts lecturing me about this now...with all that had just happened...*

"What are you going to tell them?" He paused, actually waiting to hear her answer, not just to let her finish so he could tell her how wrong he was. She told him of her plans to stay in Dogwood and maybe build a house on Paw's land, and of her uncertainty about where to look for work next.

Monroe heard her out, and nodded thoughtfully. "You know what you'd be good at?"

"Don't start with the whole med school thing, Dad."

He held up a hand to silence her. "No, that's not what I was going to say at all, Claire. I was just thinking that you might like to do in-home healthcare. That seems like an area you'd be especially good at. Most of the patients would be elderly, I think, and you're good with older people. I just thought it was something you would enjoy."

This might have been the first time, she realized, her

father had ever made a suggestion based solely on her preferences or interests. "Thanks, Daddy. That's actually a really good idea. I'll look into it."

"Don't sound so surprised. I always give you good advice," Monroe said. "Try this salad. It's not half bad. Cucumbers are a little limp, but what do you expect in a hospital cafeteria? I'm gonna see if Dad wants anything." Her father left her sitting there, pondering a future that somehow seemed both more and less certain than it ever had before.

Paw entered the cafeteria amid the rattle and clank of silverware being sorted and washed in the kitchen, the racket of trays pushed along and filled with food, and the din of voices. People passed by him going this way and that, looking for tables, stopping at the various food bars. Some seemed to just be in motion for its own sake.

It was obvious by the look on his face that the chaos of noise and movement set his already sensitive nerves to jangling and he was relieved to spot her in the corner booth. He slid in across from her and ran his fingers through his hair for the umpteenth time. His cap was in his hands, and although it would've been an improvement over the wild gray tangle on his head, Claire knew that it was practically against his religion to wear a cap indoors. He carried it now as a comfort, something familiar amid all the newness, the newness of a world where his Millie was mortal.

"I think the cheeseburgers are alright. Want one?" Claire ventured. Paw nodded mutely. When she returned with his meal, he ate mechanically, then began carefully folding the burger's foil wrapper into tiny squares. That done, Paw finally began to speak.

"Monroe was telling me about you wanting to buy an acre from us, maybe build you a little house."

Claire was a touch annoyed her father had once again put his nose in her business, but it wasn't the time for pettiness. "We don't have to talk about this right now, Paw."

"No, I want to. I think it's a good idea. I'd really appreciate having you close, in case, you know. Something else might happen." He swallowed and looked down at the table. "Can I ask you for a favor?"

"Anything," Claire said. She wished with all her heart her grandfather was the kind of man who could take a hug

139

when one was needed. But he wasn't, and she knew it, so she sat and waited for him to speak.

"Would you consider moving in with us for a little while? I know you'd rather have a place of your own, but it might be for your good. Financially, I mean. 'Til you get on your feet and all that." Someone walking by dropped a tray. The crash interrupted Paw's words, but only for a moment. He leaned across the table. Claire did the same.

"We need you there. Don't tell your Gran. She don't think she needs anybody, but I know better."

Claire started to assure Paw that Gran would be back to her old self very soon. He interrupted. "She'll be fine but she'll be better with her girl nearby." He leaned back again. "If you don't want to, I understand and I won't be mad. I just wanted to make the offer. We're kinda used to havin' you around."

Claire smiled, and blinked hard. They were tears of love and gratitude, but she had done enough crying for one day. She was going to keep these back, no matter what.

"OK, Paw. I'll stay as long as you need me to."

Paw nodded, relieved. "Better get back up there."

****

Claire made her way to her grandmother's hospital room, carefully balancing the stack of things from home Gran had requested. At the top of the list had been her own pillow. It might be lumpy, flat, and hard, but it was hers and it was comforting. She had also whispered in Claire's ear to bring "my denture things." It was a secret more closely guarded than Fort Knox that her grandmother wore dentures. Only Paw and Claire had ever seen the little box Gran called the Chopper Hopper, where her false teeth spent their nights. She also had a change of clothes for herself and Paw, who showed no intention of leaving the hospital room until he had his Millie with him.

Claire approached room 483 and noticed the door was slightly open. She peeked in to see if Gran was still sleeping. Her father had gone home for the night and Paw was stretched out asleep in a semi-reclining chair next to the window. Gran was wide awake and talking in low tones. Claire pushed the door open a crack further and saw Jake Weston sitting next to Gran's head.

Although she couldn't make out the words, she could

tell Gran was having a very serious talk with her pastor. She stood rooted to the spot, not wanting to attract any attention to herself. Talking to Jake now was out of the question.

Gran and Jake bowed their heads to pray together and Claire seized the opportunity. She laid her armful of stuff by the door, backed down the hallway slowly, then turned and hurried into the nearest restroom, where she waited until she felt sure Jake would be gone.

Paw must have called and told him what happened. She should've known he would come. What else would a good pastor do?

Sitting on the toilet in the first stall, Claire thought how awful it was to hate such a wonderful man. A man of God at that!

Maybe I don't really hate him...No, I'm pretty sure I do. The sound of a toilet flushing reminded her she was hiding in a bathroom and sent her back on her original errand, trailing a piece of toilet paper from her heel. She discovered it halfway back to Gran's room, and thought it was appropriate, since she felt pretty much like something that had been stepped on.

****

Claire spent the night on a cot, listening to the beeping of monitors and the duet of Paw's rumbling snores mixing with Gran's whistling ones. No one slept for very long at a time. Paw didn't seem to trust the nurses to take care of Gran properly, but when Claire promised to keep an eye on things, she was finally able to convince him to go home and get some rest.

On the second morning of their stay, the sunshine began calling to her, warming her face and luring her out of the chilly hospital room. Gran was resting, Paw had gone home to tend to the cattle and the garden and her father was at work. Since no one needed her at the moment, Claire decided to take a short walk.

She had just stepped out of the front door when she was met with an outstretched walking stick. Mrs. Lola Faye stood before her, accompanied by her son.

Jesse smiled at the look of shock on Claire's face. "Long time no-see," he said.

She tried to think of something casual to say, but

nothing came to mind except half questions. How did? When? What happened?

Mrs. Lola Faye was ready and willing to fill in the blanks for her.

"Claire, I swear, it scared me to death when I heard about Millie. It's all over Dogwood now. Don't worry, I got the prayer chain started myself. The preacher come over and told me the day it happened. But I'm just now getting up here because he hadn't no more got gone than, lo and behold, Jesse shows up. He told me about you and the preacher comin' to his house. I ain't never even been to his house! Then when he told me about Deloris and Joshua…"

Mrs. Lola Faye's rapid-fire delivery faltered, her voice broke, and tears came to her eyes. She lifted her glasses, brushed them away, and poked a few hair pins back into the little ball on top of her head.

While the stream of words was dammed up, Claire took the chance to say, "Let's sit down somewhere in the shade." Mrs. Lola Faye and Jesse followed her to the benches that lined the front of the hospital. Newly discharged patients waiting for their rides surrounded them as cars pulled up and loaded their charges, ready to take them to their homes and all things familiar.

Mrs. Lola Faye sat close to Claire and, seeing that there were strangers nearby, lowered her voice slightly. "It was almost more than I could get my mind around. I was mad at first. Mad at Deloris, for sure. But I was mad at Jesse, too. Can't really tell you why I was mad at him, but I was. And then I was just sad that I'd lost so much time with Joshua, not knowing him and all. Then I got to thinking that this is a blessing, it just showed up later and came wrapped up in a little different package than I'd thought. Nobody's told Joshua yet. They're gonna ease into it, let him get to know Jesse as a friend of his mother's first before just springing it on him that he's his daddy. So, that means I've gotta wait a little while longer before I get to be the grandmother."

She stopped again, and watched a woman being wheeled to a waiting minivan. Her new baby was swaddled tightly and clutched even more tightly in her arms. The nervous father sat behind the wheel as a nurse helped mom into the backseat and baby into a car seat to set off on their first trip as a family of three. "But I think it's for the best. It certainly is a lot to get a handle on, I can tell you that."

Claire looked at Jesse, who was calmly listening to his mother talk. She wanted desperately to know where things stood with him and Deloris, but didn't want to pry. Fortunately, Jesse had inherited his mother's tendency for sharing and volunteered the information.

"I guess you're probably wondering what happened. I didn't give you and Brother Weston any clue what I was planning to do when y'all left. But that was only because I didn't know myself. Well, you probably hadn't been gone five minutes when I just got in my truck and started driving. I didn't really have a plan. I was just driving but it seemed like every way I turned was leading back to Dogwood. So I went. I prayed while I drove. I told God I was angry that so much time had gone by with me having a son and neither of us knowing the other one existed. Then this verse came to my mind out of nowhere. 'I will restore unto you the years the locusts have eaten,' and I felt like it was His way of telling me He would make it all right, even with the lost years. He would bring me and my son together now and it would be OK, one way or the other. He'll work it out for the good. I know He will."

"And Deloris?" Claire ventured, cautiously.

Jesse looked thoughtful. "We'll just have to see where that goes. Neither one of us ever filed for divorce, so that's gotta mean something right there. We're gonna have to get to know each other again." He chuckled. "Odd to say about someone you've been married to for years, but in a way, it's almost like meeting someone new. I'm willing to give it a try. She asked me to forgive her and I have. I asked her to do the same for me, so we could start over fresh. Sometimes it's hard to know you're really forgiven. It takes a lot of showing and doing, not just saying."

He looked at Claire with an open, honest gaze. "Thank you for coming to Mountain View. You've given me a great blessing. I've spent the last few days with Joshua, and he's a fine, fine boy. I'm so glad you and Brother Weston were willing to help Deloris like you did."

Mrs. Lola Faye, sitting between Jesse and Claire, squeezed them each on the knee and said, "Well now! We better get up and see Millie and get headed back home. You know you can't get around this town when people are on their lunch hours. They're all crazy anyway, but when they're *hungry* and crazy," She threw her hands up in despair of ever making it home alive, gathered her walking stick, and stood up. "You coming, Claire?"

"No, ma'am," Claire replied. "I'm just going to head home for a few hours. I need to rest and it's hard to do in a hospital room."

"Don't I know it, Lord, don't I know it!" Mrs. Lola Faye called as she and Jesse shuffled away. "All them nurses comin' in, pokin' and proddin' and worryin' you to death. A sick person can't get well for them pesterin' you night and day. No offense, Honey. I know it's your job but mercy, it gets aggravating." The automatic doors swept shut behind them, closing her off from hearing the rest of Mrs. Lola Faye's diatribe against the nursing profession. She smiled to herself as she watched Jesse carefully guide his mother, who was still talking ninety to nothing, onto an elevator and out of sight.

Chapter Sixteen

It was a rare, summer morning, not too hot, with just enough breeze to lift the stray curls away from Claire's face. She was sitting on top of the hill, her hill, where she would build her own home. *Someday.* Paw had agreed it would be a perfect house spot, whenever she was ready.

She hugged her knees to her chest and smiled at the thought. A tiny butterfly exactly the color of a lilac blossom lit on her bare foot, tricked by the bright pink toenail polish into believing it had found a new flower. Discovering its mistake, the butterfly flicked its wings and relocated to a nearby red clover blossom.

Gran would be coming home tomorrow and Paw said she'd be mad as an old wet hen when she saw how the garden had been let go in her absence. Claire sensed a good many hours of picking, snapping, shelling, washing, and canning in her future. That was fine with her. She almost looked forward to it. She was definitely looking forward to starting her search for work in the home health-care field. The staff at St. Bernadette's had been helpful in their suggestions of likely places to begin.

Jasper Johnson hadn't been the least disturbed by Claire's phone call. He was used to such news. He'd wished her luck and she was sure he had immediately begun digging through his files for another candidate.

Rita Sparks had been somewhat less supportive when she'd seen Claire in the hall and asked when she'd be moving to Dallas. Rita had been "shocked", her exact word, complete with eyebrows arched like a cat's back to verify the emotion, and a tad bit disgusted with Claire's lack of drive and her "willingness to settle." She'd reprimanded Claire for making such poor use of her connections.

Right now, Claire knew exactly which connections she needed most. But with all her feelings of contentment and peace, there was one uneasy spot in her heart, one nagging feeling that wouldn't be eased. As good as she felt about her decisions, not being able to talk to Jake about everything troubled her. What was even worse was he had no idea she was angry with him. Hurt by him was more like it. She knew she'd have to face him eventually. Claire mulled it all over for the hundredth time as she walked slowly toward the house.

"Claire," She heard Jake call her name from the front porch swing. *He sounds nervous.* Probably because her avoiding him during his hospital visits to Gran had become more and more obvious.

"Hi," she returned tentatively. "Gran hasn't come home yet. She'll be released tomorrow morning."

Claire settled herself on the top step and stared down the sidewalk. The porch swing chains gave a rattle as Jake relocated and sat down beside her.

"I know. I came to find you."

"Oh. Well, I guess you know about Jesse. I'm praying for them all. It'll work out, I just know it will. Mrs. Lola Faye's excited about getting to know Joshua better." Her voice trailed off with Jake watching her intently.

"I talked to Jesse just yesterday. I've got high hopes for that family, too. All of them," he said.

Jake cleared his throat and drew a deep breath.

Claire cut him off. "I want to thank you. For the advice, but mainly for listening and being such a good...friend." She almost choked on the last word. "I finally decided what to do about moving and all."

"Mrs. Millie told me."

Claire nodded, for once glad Gran had done the talking for her.

A mockingbird plummeted from one of the oak trees and landed weightlessly on the sidewalk. It snatched a June bug and was gone in a flash of gray and white. Claire could barely see it through the emerald canopy as it returned to the hungry little ones in its nest.

"You know, they do have a song of their own," Jake said. "It's not as beautiful as some of the other birds. You don't hear it very often but they've got one, just the same. I think most people don't know that."

Claire kept her eyes lifted to the treetops, avoiding Jake's gaze. He shifted uncomfortably, then plunged into speech like a man leaping off a waterfall.

"I know you came to the church the other day...the day when...someone was there."

He had her full attention now. He pushed ahead quickly, not giving her time to speak.

"I saw you drive away. I've wanted to say something ever since, to explain. I owe you an explanation. But with Mrs. Millie's heart attack, I thought it just wasn't the right time and, then I thought you might, I don't know." He rubbed his chin, flustered. It caused her a little stab of pain to see him so ill-at-ease, so unlike himself.

"You don't have to explain anything to me. You have every right to..." she hunted for the right word, "...*see* any woman you want."

"But that's just it. I knew this was what had happened. I knew you'd misinterpreted. Well, at least you misinterpreted my part of it." He seemed desperate for her to understand.

"When Miranda came to my office, she said she needed spiritual counseling. For a personal matter. She didn't say what, and the more she talked, the more I suspected she wasn't really there to be counseled. But I'm so *dense*, I honestly couldn't figure what she wanted."

He gave himself a firm knuckling to the forehead before continuing. "I thought maybe she was just lonely. But when I tried to walk her out, she...she tried to kiss me."

Delight and surprise registered on Claire's face for just a split second before she recomposed the expressionless mask she'd been working to create.

"Tried?"

"*Tried.* But I backed away and told her, well, that nothing in *that way* was going to happen."

"How'd she take that?" Claire couldn't help asking.

Jake allowed himself a wry half-smile. "She probably won't be joining us for Worship this Sunday."

"Let me ask you something," Claire said, unable to keep a slight edge from her voice. "How could you not see what she was up to? I've known Miranda Davenport was after you since I came to Dogwood."

"Because," he said quietly, "when a man has his heart set on a certain woman, it's like no others exist."

The blood rushed to Claire's face and pounded in her

ears. She tried to make a grab at the swarm of emotions that swirled through her brain and gather them into one cohesive something...something that could be formed into sensible words. No such luck.

Jake struggled on. "I don't know how you feel and I haven't wanted to make you uncomfortable."

From the tangle in her head, Mrs. Lola Faye's words emerged. Something about not being sure what to do until you do it, then somehow *just knowing* it was right.

Her lips met his, stilling the stream of words and explanations with a kiss. Soft, gentle, hesitant, and at the same time a complete relief.

When they parted, the slow, easy grin that spread across Jake's face spoke the same emotion as the burning flush that colored Claire's. Jake took her hand in his and they sat in a wonderful, unthinking happiness for a while. Claire knew neither wanted to break the sweet quiet between them.

Claire finally said, "It's time to start dinner. You wanna stay?"

"Depends on what you're fixin'."

She pulled him to his feet. "If a country preacher is going to eat at my table, I suppose fried chicken would be in order. But since I'm taking Gran the leftovers, it'll have to be baked instead."

"I'll just stay for the good company then."

"Only if you help me wash the dishes afterwards."

"Deal," he said, dropping a kiss on her forehead. Claire breathed a contented sigh.

Jake slipped his arm around her as they passed into the little white frame house, letting the screen door scrape shut behind them.

Epilogue

"Paw, wake up!" Claire scurried into the living room and gave her grandfather a whack on the shoulder. "You too, Daddy." She hurried off to her room in a cloud of aqua chiffon. "I can't believe I forgot it!" she mumbled to herself as her high heels clicked along the hall.

Claire stopped short as she passed the mirror hanging above her dresser. Shining auburn waves cascaded down her back, and for once, she thought her hair looked lovely. She considered thanking God for this miracle of manageable hair, but decided she should probably thank Lottie instead. Those two hours of teasing, hot rollers, curling irons, and enough hairspray to choke a person had paid off.

It had been a year since she and Jake had helped reunite Jesse with his estranged wife. During the months that followed, Claire had seen the couple move from cold, formal politeness to a genuine friendship, which had blossomed into a deep, pure love. Claire had been honored when Deloris had asked her to take part in their second wedding. She could hardly believe the restoration God had worked in the Nugent family. Not only had Deloris and Jesse's marriage been put back together, but Mrs. Lola Faye had come to love her new-found daughter-in-law and grandson as if the family had never been separated. In fact, all of Dogwood Church had embraced the Nugents and encouraged Deloris in her first nervous visits to church. Now, Claire reflected, Deloris was one of the first to greet new visitors and offer to have them over for dinner. Claire expected the entire congregation to turn out for the "re-wedding," as Jesse called it.

"This time, I'm going to do things right," Deloris had said. When they'd taken pictures earlier in the day, Claire had been amazed at the transformation of the humble little church. Ivory roses filled the sanctuary with their rich, sweet aroma and mingled with the greenery adorning a wooden archway Jesse had carved especially for the occasion. Deloris, with Claire's help, had even chosen a tux for Jake to wear as he officiated the service.

Jake. Claire's heart began to pound. She couldn't wait to see him standing there at the front of the church, looking so handsome and...

She snapped out of her reverie with a gasp. *Get it together, Claire*, she chided herself.

She rummaged around in the top dresser drawer until her fingers found a small, velvet bag. Inside was a wide gold wedding band with the day's date engraved inside it. Next to the date were the words "Love Never Fails." Claire slipped the velvet bag inside her small beaded purse. She took a deep breath, exhaled with a prayer of thanks, and hurried off to gather her family for the short drive to the church.

****

"I still don't see why we all had to ride together," Monroe grumbled gently as he peered out the back window of the trusty old Buick.

"I just thought it would be nice," Claire replied, breathlessly. She smoothed the soft material of her flowing dress again and again as she looked at her father with a nervous smile.

"Breathe, Claire Bear," her father said as he encircled her freckled shoulders with his strong arm. "You look so nervous, you'd think it was your wedding day. Relax! All you have to do is just stand there and look beautiful." He dropped a kiss on the top of her head. "That won't be a problem."

Claire fought back a wave of tears and squeezed her father's shoulder. "Don't make me ruin this makeup," she said with a wobbly smile. Her father gave her a bemused look as they pulled into the church's gravel parking lot.

Paw, Gran, and Monroe took their place in the line of people who were slowly filing into the church. Claire hurried to a side door that led into the tiny nursery, which was serving as the bride's room.

She found Deloris sitting calmly in her wheelchair, a wide smile lighting her face. Sage Finley, the other bridesmaid, was busily applying blush to the bride's cheeks. Sage and Deloris had made fast friends after Sage discovered they both had a penchant for Jane Austen's novels and Tex-Mex restaurants.

"Sage, dear, if you put any more blush on me I'll look as though I'm about to have a heat stroke. Or I'll look like Claire when she's nervous." Deloris gestured toward the bright red hives that were creeping along Claire's neck. She gave Claire a conspiratorial wink. "Good thing we did the pictures before you had a chance to work yourself into one solid red blotch."

Before Claire had a chance to respond, a tuxedo-clad Joshua burst in the door. "It's time, Momma!" he said, deftly maneuvering Deloris's chair out into the narrow hall that led to the foyer with Sage and Claire following behind.

****

Claire nudged open the double doors that led into the sanctuary and surveyed the crowd. The small church was full. She saw Paw, Gran, and her father wedged tightly together on a middle pew.

"Surely it's almost time to start, isn't it?" she asked as she fidgeted with the bouquet of pink roses in her hand. Sage looked at her curiously. "We're waiting for the men to come in. That's the signal, remember?"

The side door at the front of the auditorium opened and Jesse strode to the front of the church. His usually shaggy blonde beard was trimmed and his unruly hair had been tamed as well. He looked downright dapper.

"Oh, Deloris..." Claire began to say how handsome her husband looked, but she stopped short.

Jake was taking his place beside Jesse. For a brief second, Jake's eyes met Claire's. He gave her a tiny smile and she was almost sure she saw him wink. In that same instant, the organ began playing. Sage pushed passed Claire and started up the aisle. Within seconds, Claire followed. Once at the front of the church, they turned and faced the crowd as The Bridal March began to play.

Deloris began wheeling down the aisle, a radiant smile on her face. Joshua held her hand as they progressed slowly toward Jesse.

When they reached the front, Joshua stepped back and Jesse took his wife's hand. He knelt and kissed it, then rose again as they turned to face Jake.

"I know this isn't a commonly used wedding passage, but at the request of the groom, let me share Joel 2:25 with y'all." Jake's voice was steady, strong and joyous. As the ceremony progressed, Claire's jittery feelings ebbed away and she listened to Jake's words with peace and wonder. She touched the gold ring, which she had tied to the ribbons on her bouquet.

"You may kiss your bride," Jake said as the church erupted into applause.

Jesse and Deloris turned to face the crowd, both beaming, and crying. But instead of hurrying down the aisle together, they simply moved to the side and waited. Joshua, who clearly didn't know this was unusual wedding behavior, sat down in his mother's lap.

Next to Claire, Sage leaned over and whispered, "Why aren't they leaving?"

Claire didn't seem to hear her. She was moving toward Jake, who had his hand outstretched. She grasped his strong hand in hers and held on as if she'd never let go.

"Did you get the ring?" he whispered, his breath lifting an escaped tendril off her neck. The congregation had fallen silent. Claire nodded, and they faced the confused guests.

An elderly gentleman in a suit sat on the end of the front pew. Jake motioned to him and the man came forward, cleared his throat, and took his place next to the pastor.

"Well, folks, you're getting more than you bargained for. It's a two for one wedding day here at Dogwood Community Church." The applause that had so recently died down sprung back to life with renewed vigor.

Claire could see Gran's eyes grow big with surprise for just a moment before the tears of joy came. Next to her, Paw nodded approvingly. Her father's face registered shock, then briefly annoyance. He met his daughter's worried gaze, shook his finger at her, and started to smile. Since she and Jake had concocted their crazy plan at Deloris's suggestion just a week ago, she'd wondered how her family would react. The last thing she wanted was a big, society-page wedding, which she knew her father would insist upon. Gran would likely regret not getting to boss her around as they planned a wedding together, but Claire knew Paw would be delighted to be spared having to listen to all the hashing and rehashing of decoration details and reception menus.

The riotous clapping finally subsided, and Jake continued speaking. "Brother Glover, who pastors Claire's home church, has graciously agreed to officiate."

Brother Glover opened his Bible and addressed the couple. "James 1:17 tells us every good and perfect gift comes down from the Father of the Heavenly Lights, in whom there is no shadow of turning. Jake and Claire, your love for each other is a gift from God," Brother Glover said. In the front row, Claire heard Mrs. Lola Faye softly say "Amen." Brother Glover looked at Jake. "Brother Weston, I've known Claire Burke since she was a just a little girl. She's a fine woman, and I charge you to remember the words of Proverbs 18:22. 'He who finds a wife finds what is good, and receives favor from the Lord.'" It was Jake's turn to say "Amen," as he gave Claire's hand a squeeze.

The rest of the service was like a dream to Claire, beautiful and unreal. In just a few moments, she heard Brother Glover say "I now present to you the Reverend and Mrs. Jake Weston. Jake, you may kiss your bride."

Jake cupped Claire's face in his hands. "I love you," she said, looking into the honey colored eyes that were slowly filling with tears. As the church members clapped and Joshua whooped and whistled, she kissed her husband.

****

"I hope everyone enjoys the reception," Claire said as they rumbled out of the church parking lot in Jake's truck. They'd made only a brief appearance in the fellowship hall after the service, where Jake had received quite a few slaps on the back, and Claire had been threatened with a whooping by both Gran and Mrs. Lola Faye.

"We certainly gave them something to talk about besides the shrimp dip, didn't we? You're sure you didn't want to stay longer?" Jake asked.

Claire snuggled against her husband. There would be time for visiting later. She was sure they'd have plenty of company in the tiny parsonage when they returned from their honeymoon and even more if the church allowed them to move into her house that was already under construction on the hill in Pa's field. For now, all she wanted was to be alone with Jake.

"I'm sure. There's a cabin in the mountains that's calling our names," she said with a sly smile. Jake slipped his arm around her shoulders. Just right, she thought. Claire switched the radio on as they headed north, leaving a cloud of dust and fiddle music hovering in the air behind them.

A word about the author...

Sarah Goodman lives and writes in Prattsville, AR, where she is surrounded by beef cattle, English Shepherds, and wild little boys. She holds a B.A. in Christian Theology and writes feature articles for a local newspaper. In her spare time, she enjoys doing Beth Moore Bible Studies, reading, writing, and—her favorite and most neglected hobby—sleeping. This is her first novel.

Printed in the United States
107805LV00008B/1-18/P